Peanut, Butter, & Crackers

Puppy Problems

PAIGE BRADDOCK

Coloring by Kat Efird

VIKING

To Buddy Barker, Otis, and Charlie—P. B.

VIKING

An imprint of Penguin Random House LLC, New York

First published in the United States of America by Viking,
an imprint of Penguin Random House LLC, 2020

Visit us online at penguinrandomhouse.com

LIBRARY OF CONGRESS CATALOGING-IN-PUBLICATION DATA IS AVAILABLE
ISBN 9780593117439

Manufactured in China

1 3 5 7 9 10 8 6 4 2

Book design by Paige Braddock and Lucia Baez

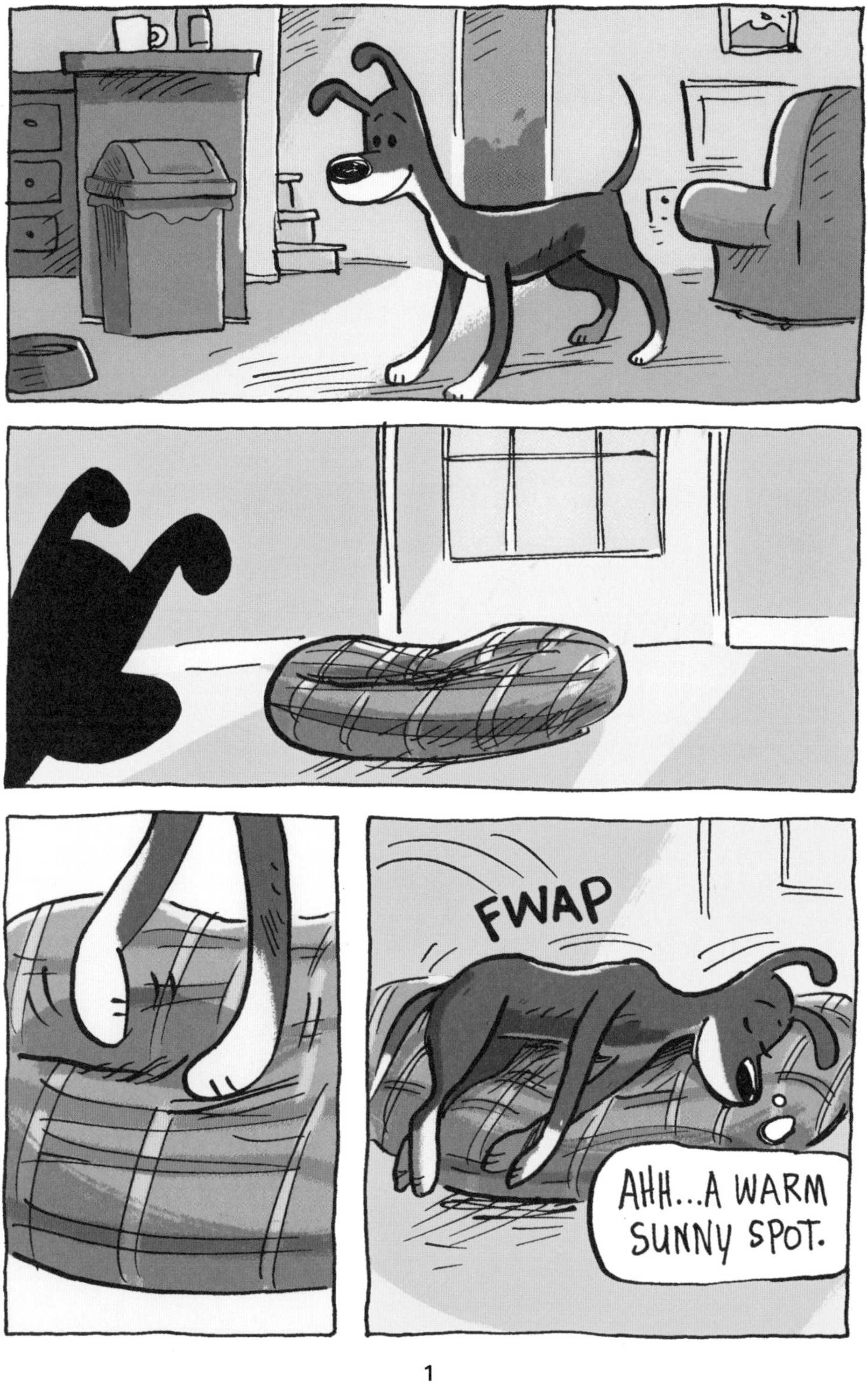
FWAP
AHH...A WARM SUNNY SPOT.

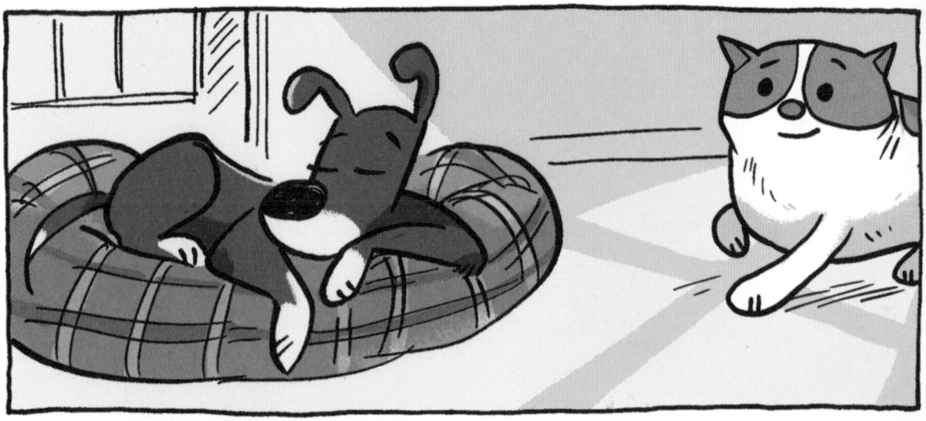

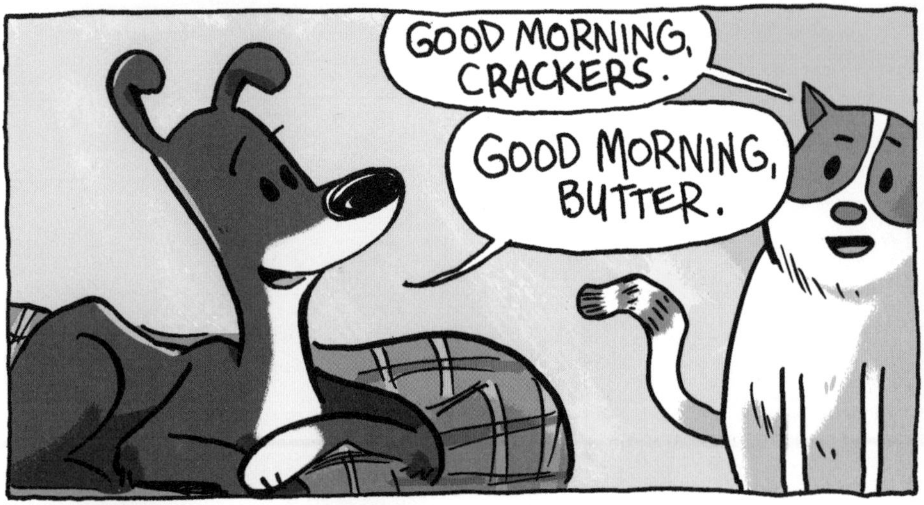
GOOD MORNING, CRACKERS.
GOOD MORNING, BUTTER.

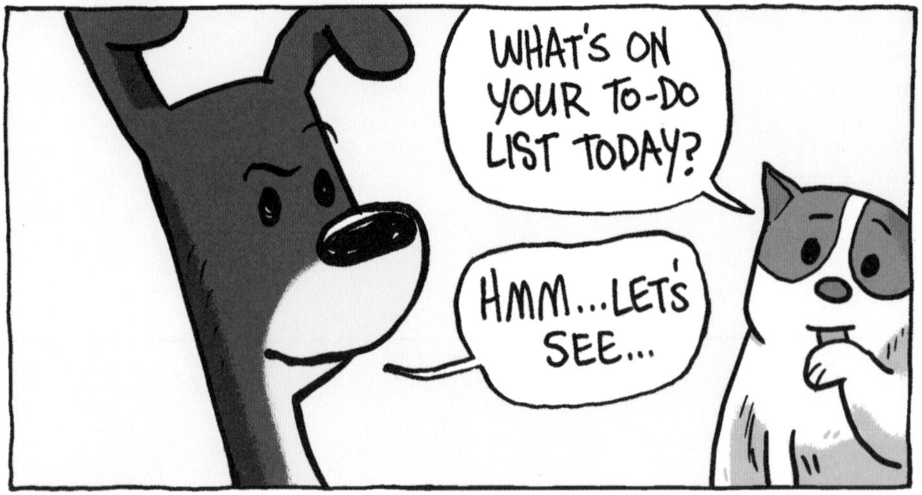
WHAT'S ON YOUR TO-DO LIST TODAY?
HMM...LET'S SEE...

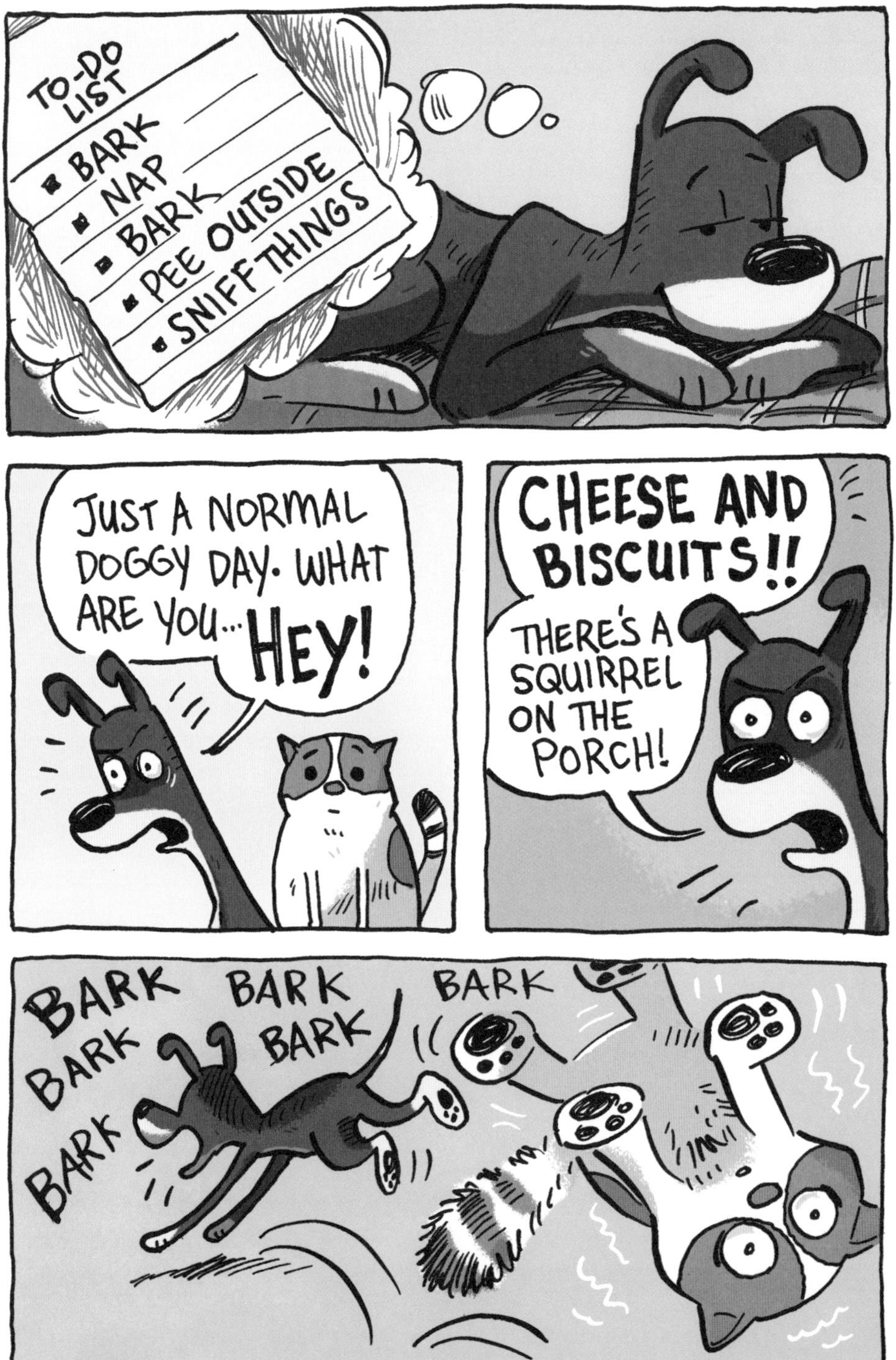
TO-DO LIST
BARK
NAP
BARK
PEE OUTSIDE
SNIFF THINGS
JUST A NORMAL DOGGY DAY. WHAT ARE YOU... HEY!
CHEESE AND BISCUITS!!
THERE'S A SQUIRREL ON THE PORCH!
BARK BARK BARK
BARK BARK
BARK

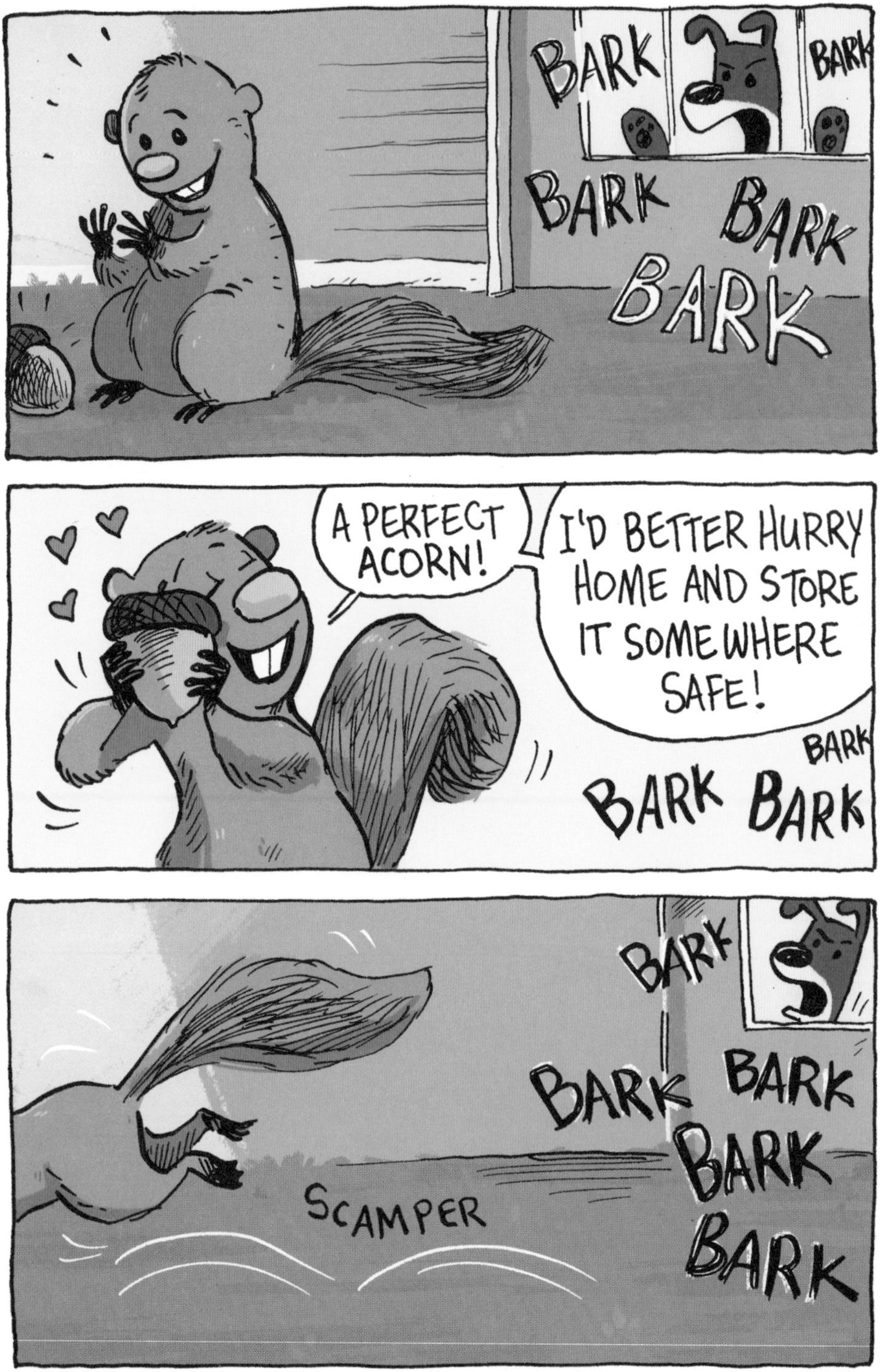
BARK
BARK
BARK
BARK
BARK
A PERFECT ACORN!
I'D BETTER HURRY HOME AND STORE IT SOMEWHERE SAFE!
BARK
BARK
BARK
BARK
BARK
BARK
BARK
BARK
SCAMPER

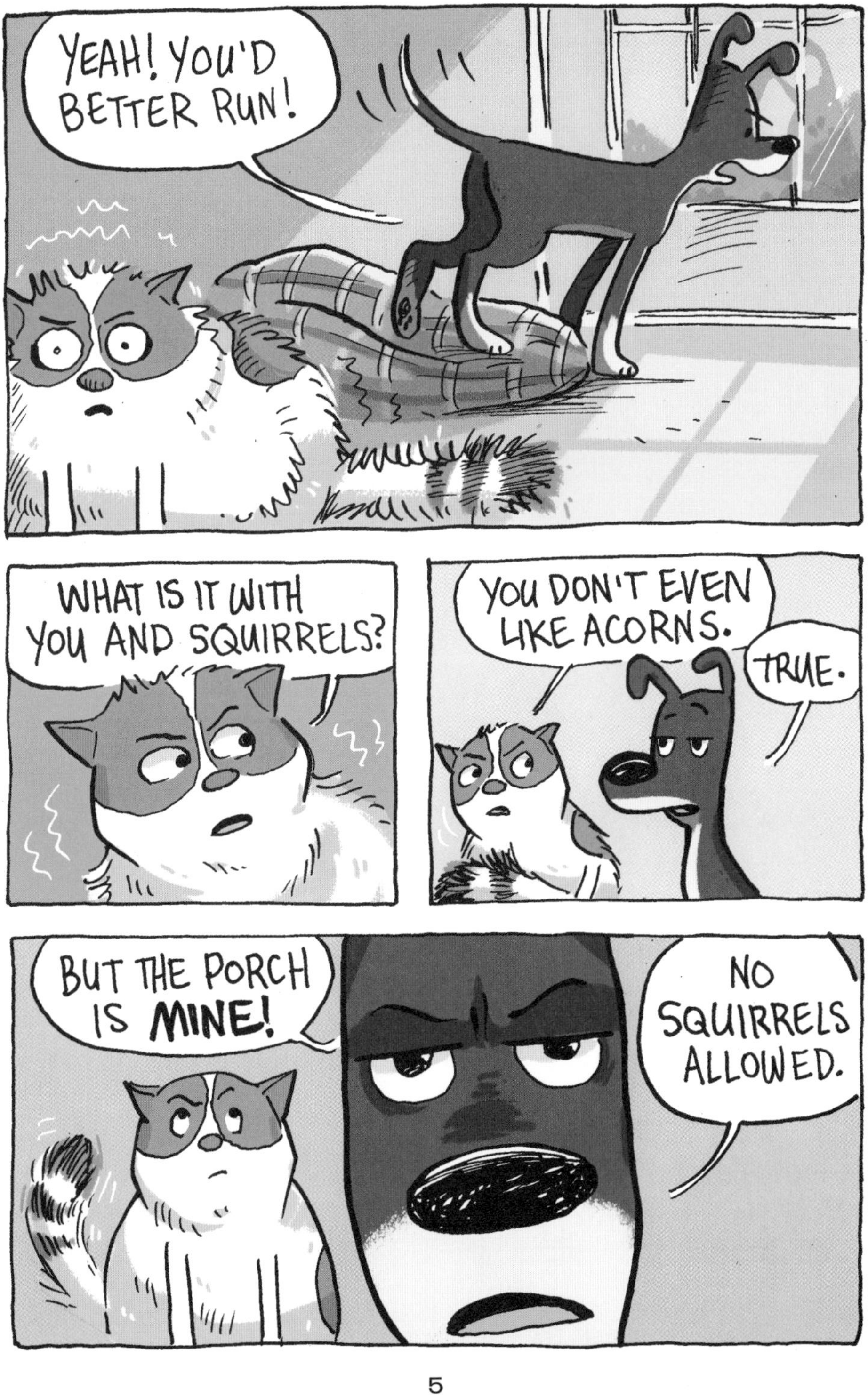
YEAH! YOU'D BETTER RUN!
WHAT IS IT WITH YOU AND SQUIRRELS?
YOU DON'T EVEN LIKE ACORNS.
TRUE.
BUT THE PORCH IS **MINE!**
NO SQUIRRELS ALLOWED.

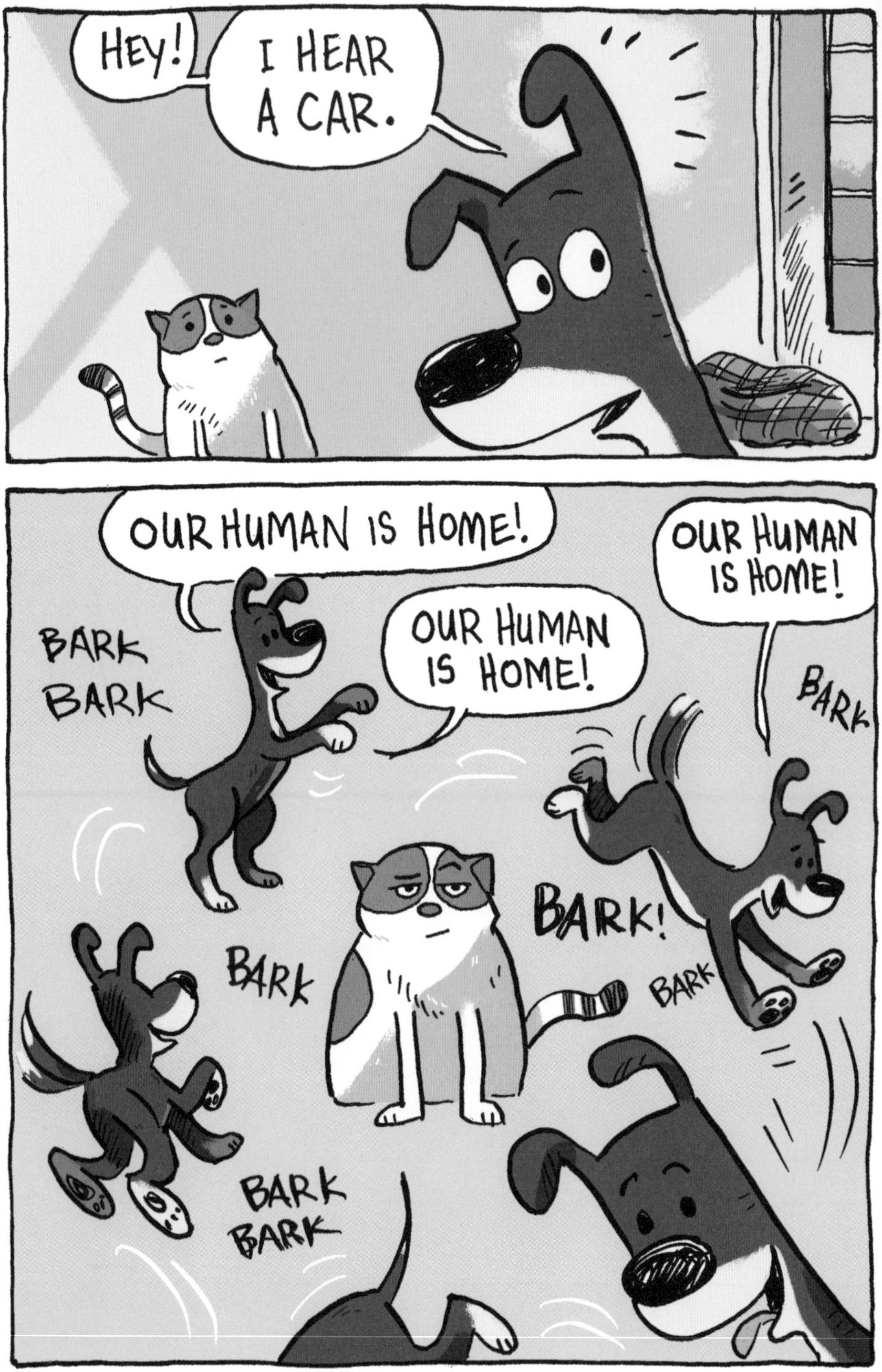
HEY!
I HEAR A CAR.
OUR HUMAN IS HOME!
BARK BARK
OUR HUMAN IS HOME!
OUR HUMAN IS HOME!
BARK
BARK!
BARK
BARK
BARK BARK

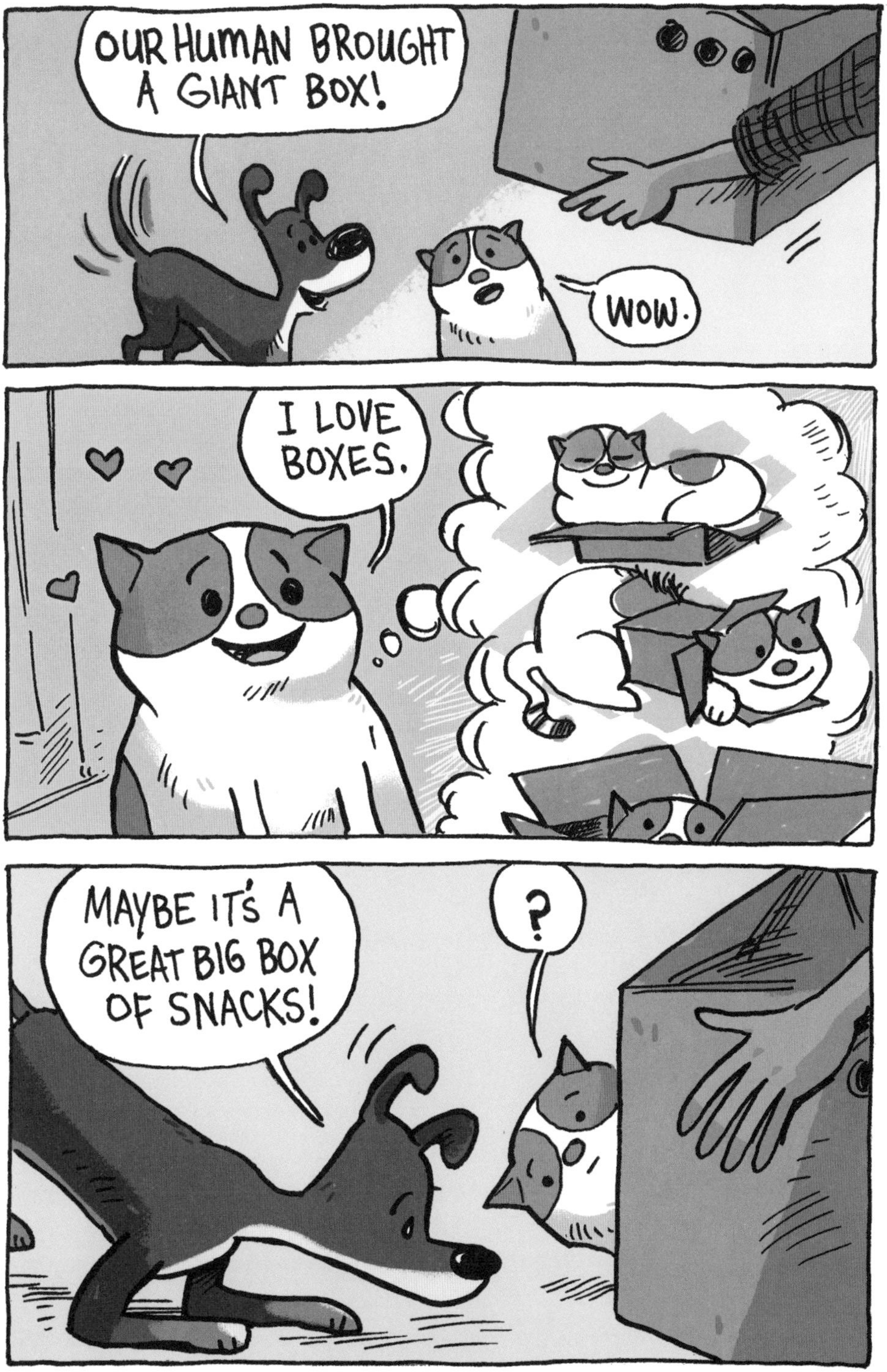
OUR HUMAN BROUGHT A GIANT BOX!
WOW.
I LOVE BOXES.
MAYBE IT'S A GREAT BIG BOX OF SNACKS!
?

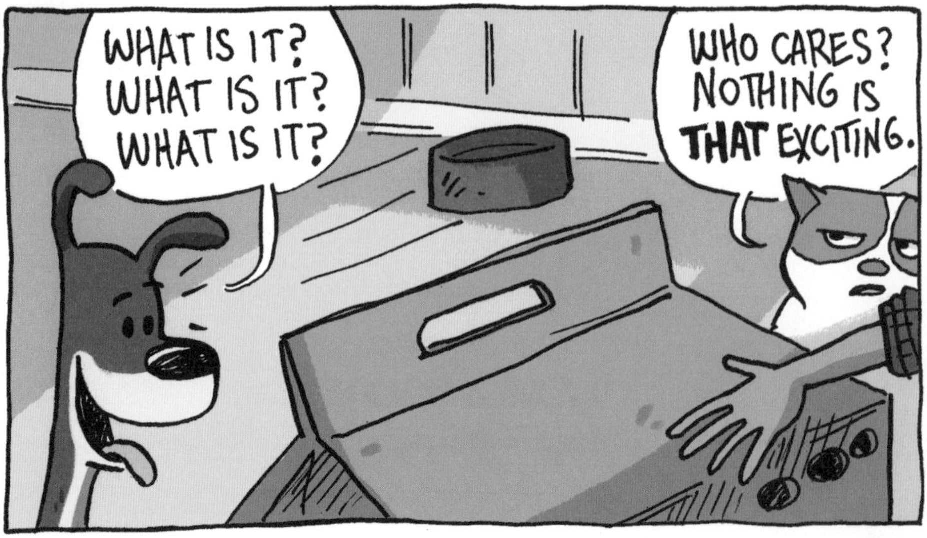
WHAT IS IT? WHAT IS IT? WHAT IS IT?
WHO CARES? NOTHING IS **THAT** EXCITING.

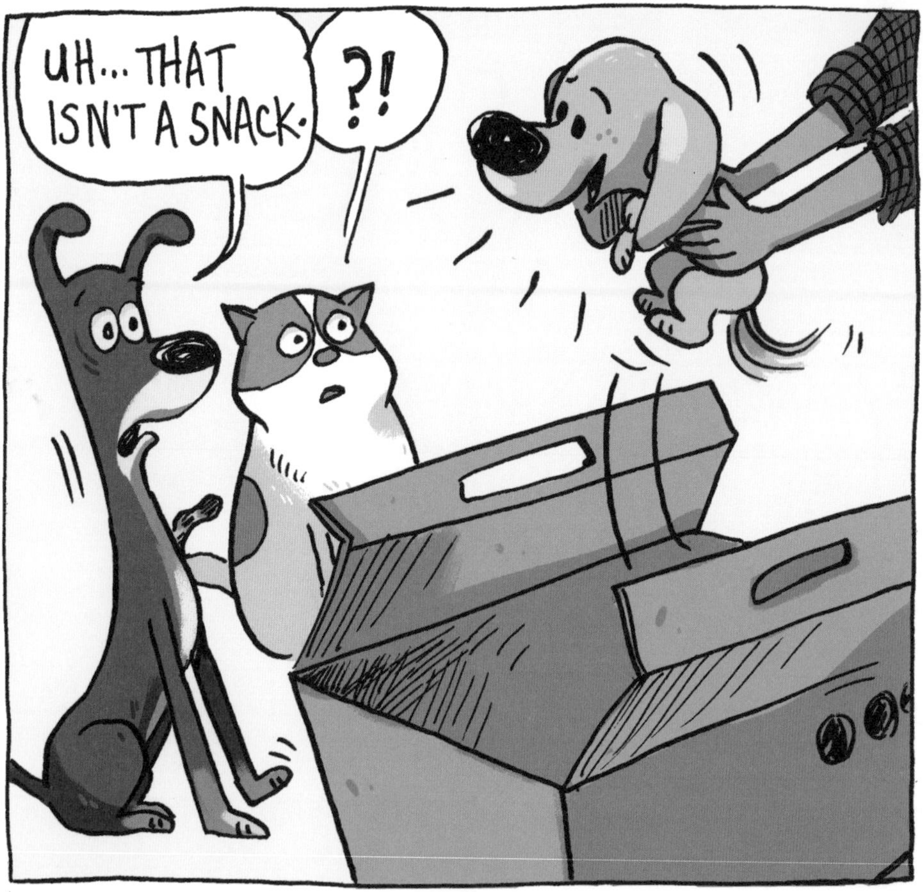
UH... THAT ISN'T A SNACK.
?!

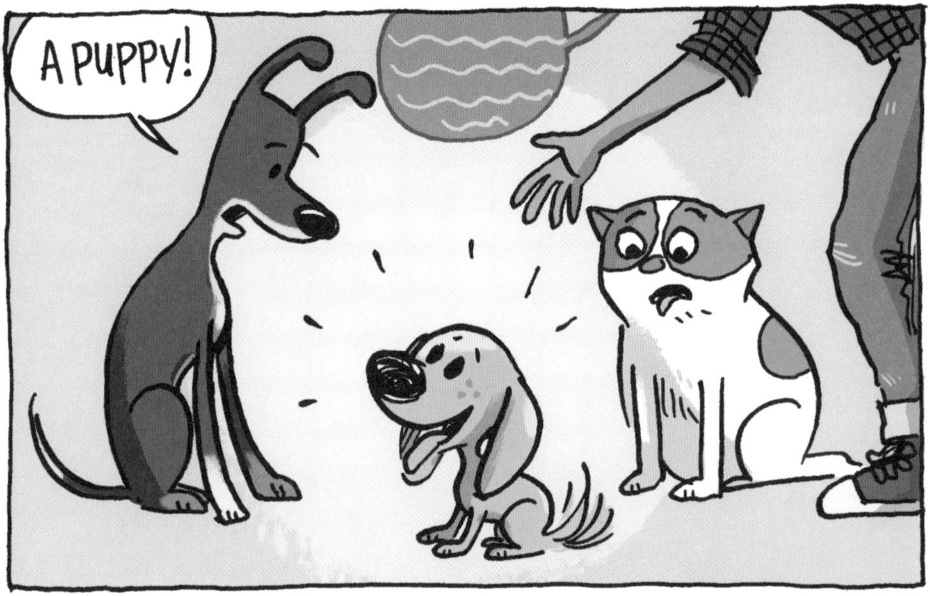
A PUPPY!

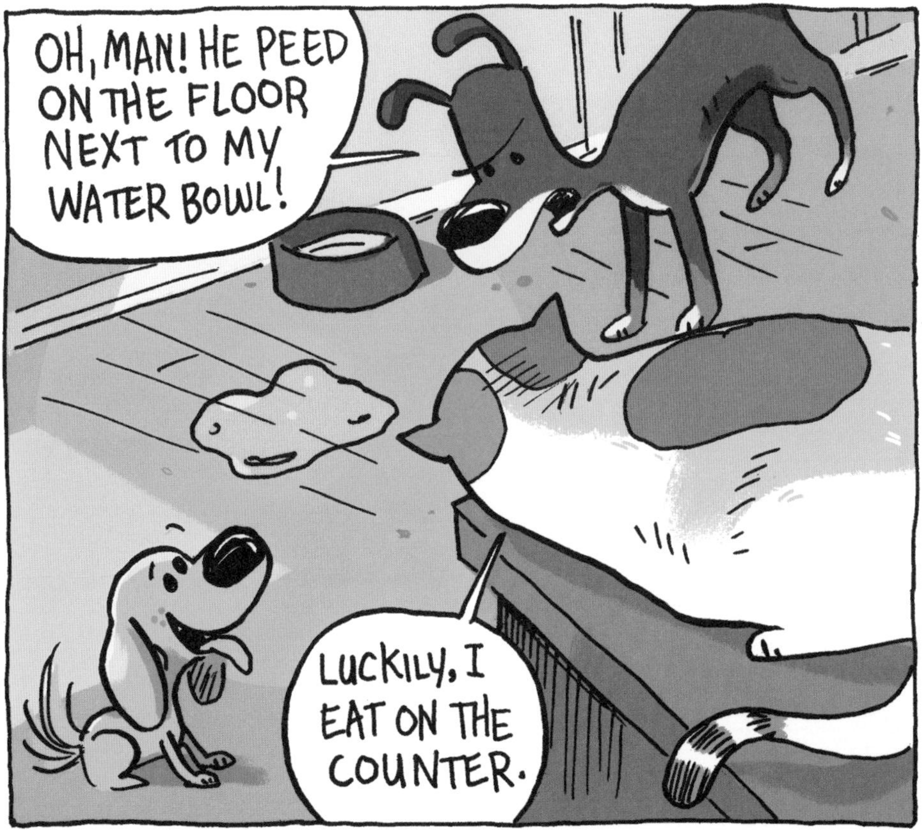
OH, MAN! HE PEED ON THE FLOOR NEXT TO MY WATER BOWL!
LUCKILY, I EAT ON THE COUNTER.

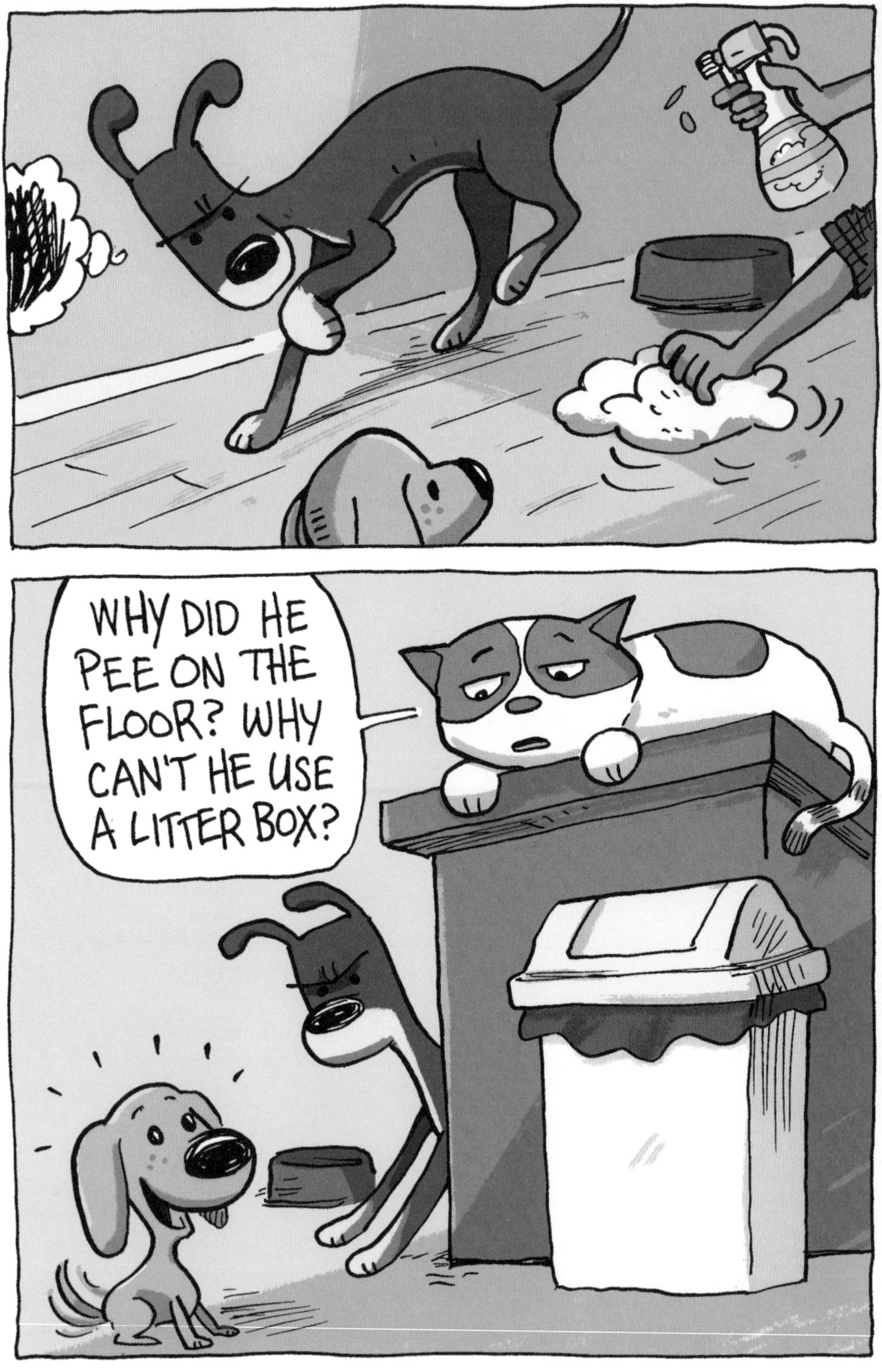
WHY DID HE PEE ON THE FLOOR? WHY CAN'T HE USE A LITTER BOX?

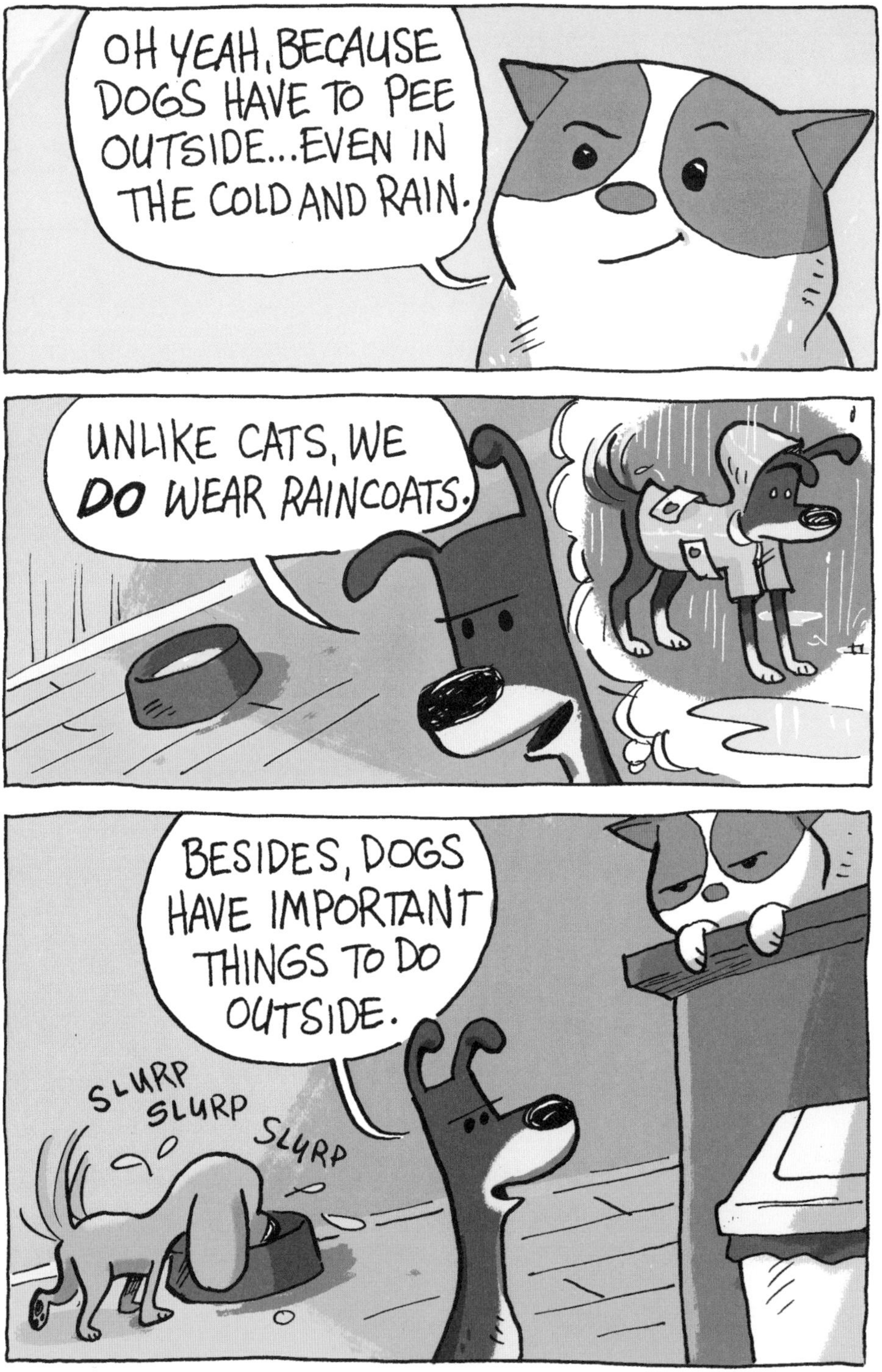
OH YEAH, BECAUSE DOGS HAVE TO PEE OUTSIDE...EVEN IN THE COLD AND RAIN.
UNLIKE CATS, WE **DO** WEAR RAINCOATS.
BESIDES, DOGS HAVE IMPORTANT THINGS TO DO OUTSIDE.
SLURP SLURP SLURP

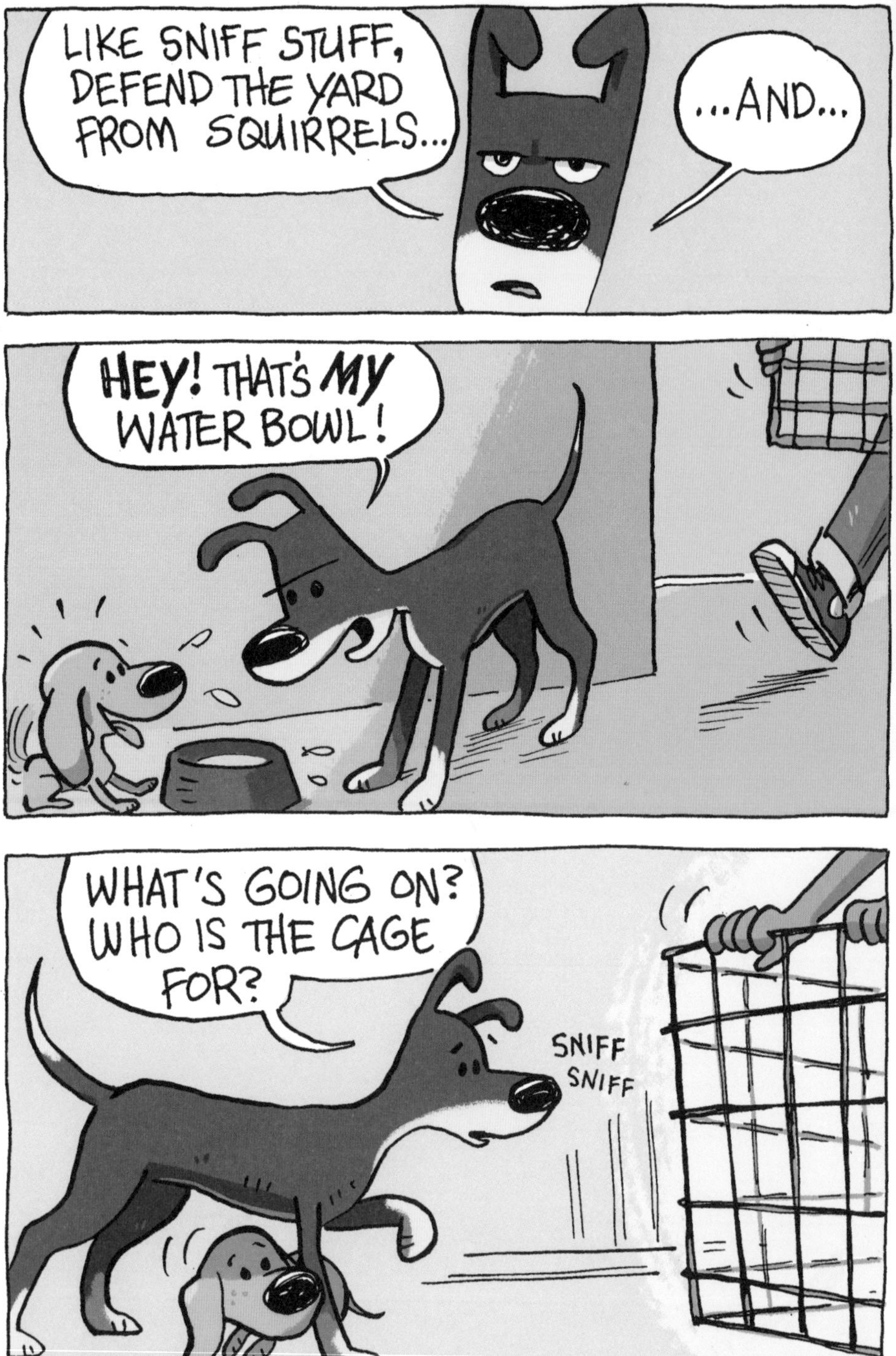
LIKE SNIFF STUFF, DEFEND THE YARD FROM SQUIRRELS...
...AND...
HEY! THAT'S MY WATER BOWL!
WHAT'S GOING ON? WHO IS THE CAGE FOR?
SNIFF SNIFF

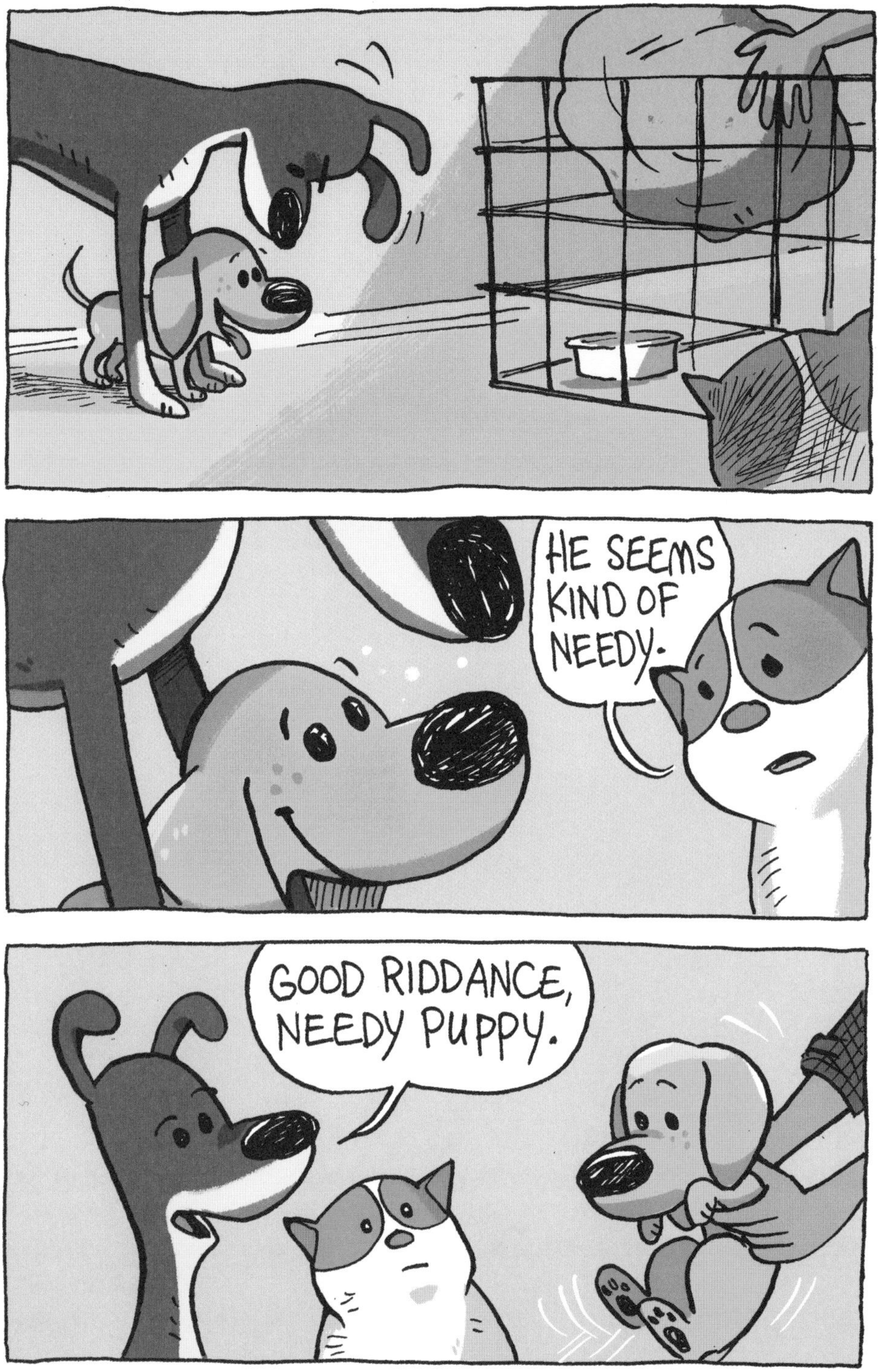
HE SEEMS KIND OF NEEDY.
GOOD RIDDANCE, NEEDY PUPPY.

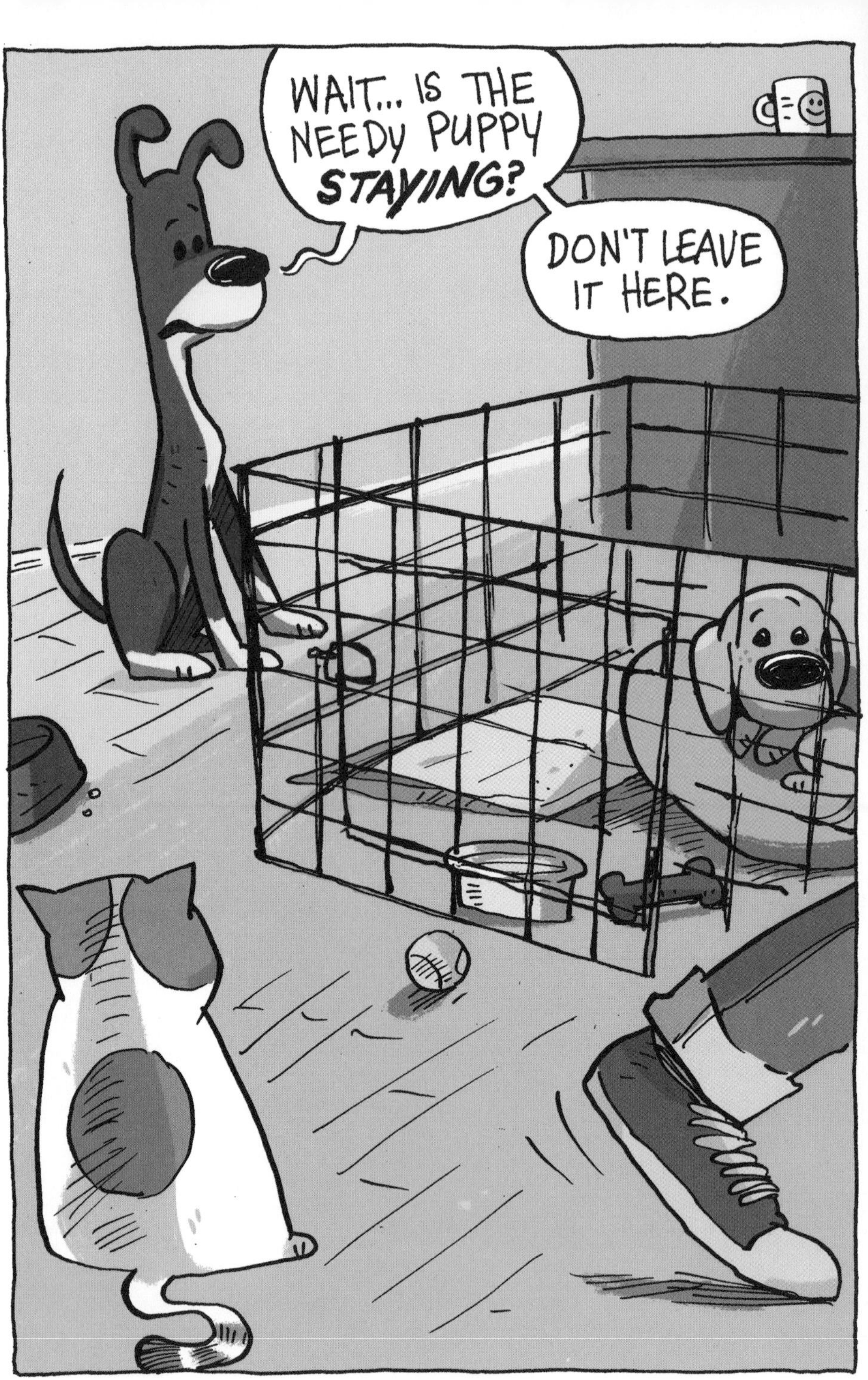
WAIT... IS THE NEEDY PUPPY STAYING?
DON'T LEAVE IT HERE.

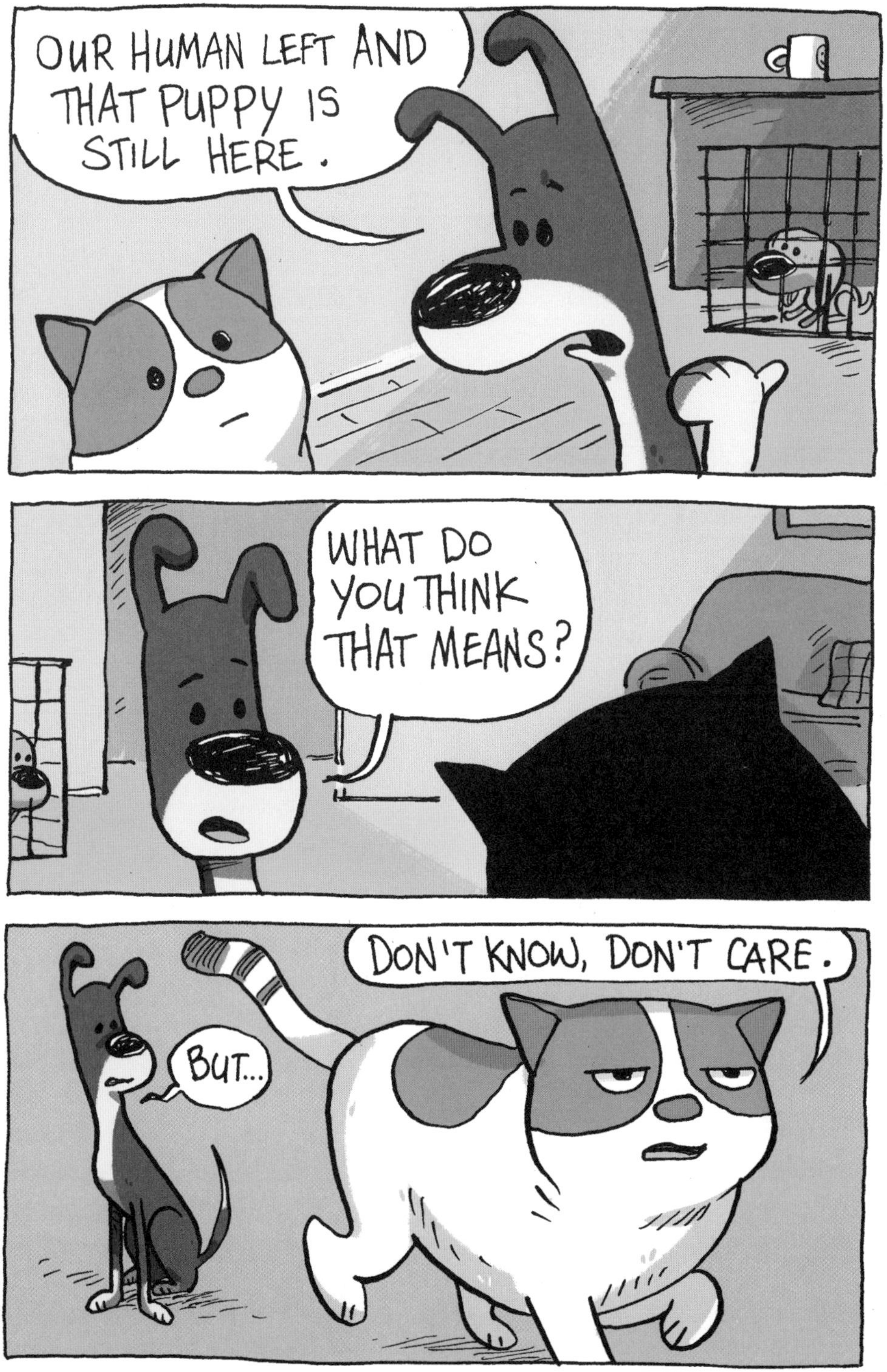
OUR HUMAN LEFT AND THAT PUPPY IS STILL HERE.
WHAT DO YOU THINK THAT MEANS?
DON'T KNOW, DON'T CARE.
BUT...

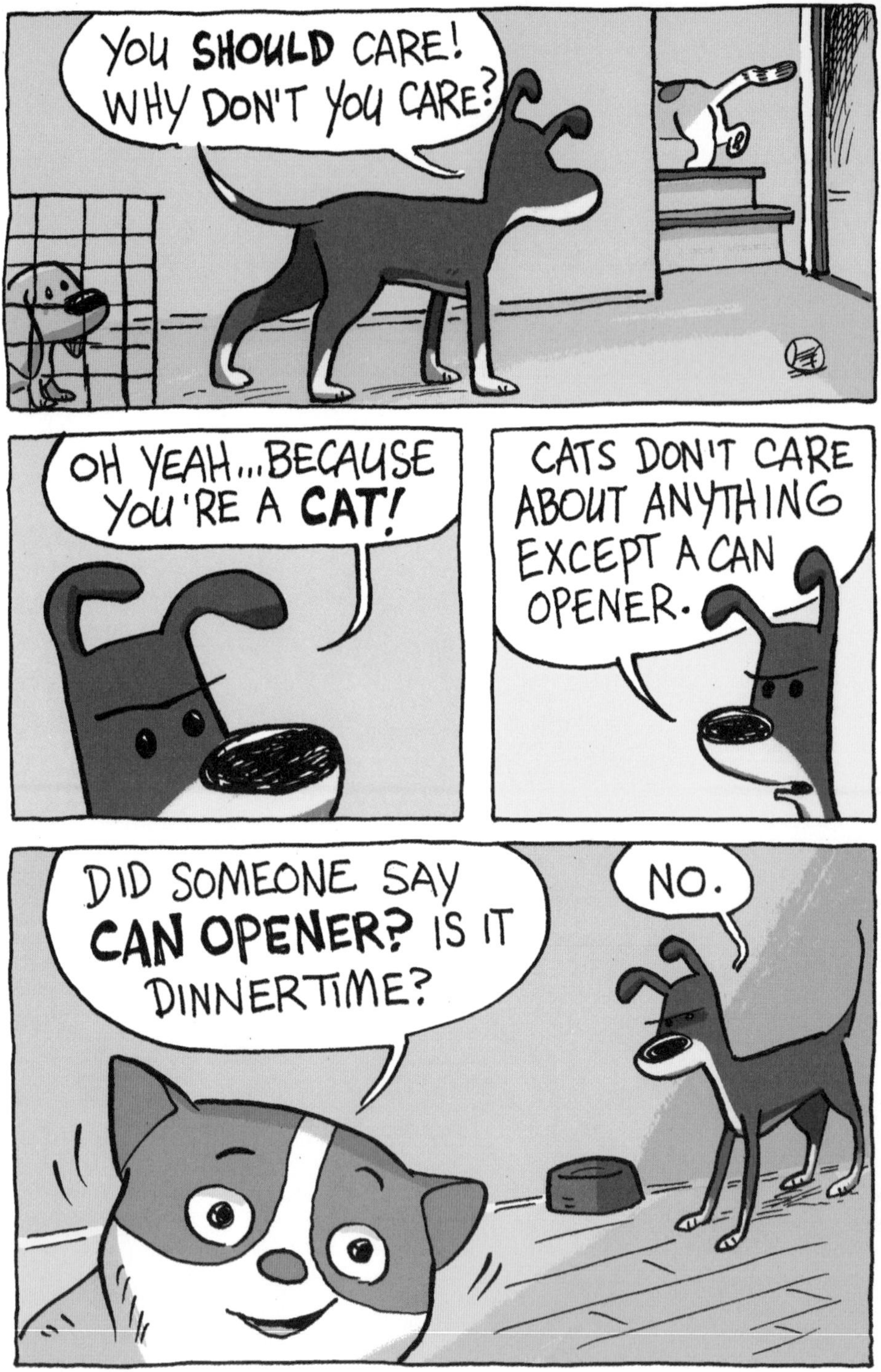
YOU **SHOULD** CARE! WHY DON'T YOU CARE?
OH YEAH...BECAUSE YOU'RE A **CAT**!
CATS DON'T CARE ABOUT ANYTHING EXCEPT A CAN OPENER.
DID SOMEONE SAY **CAN OPENER?** IS IT DINNERTIME?
NO.

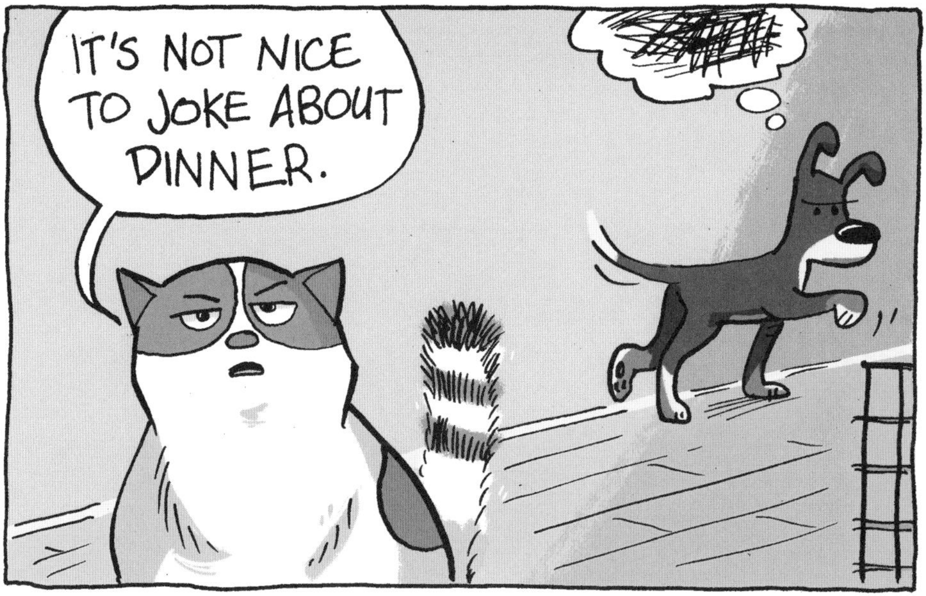
IT'S NOT NICE TO JOKE ABOUT DINNER.

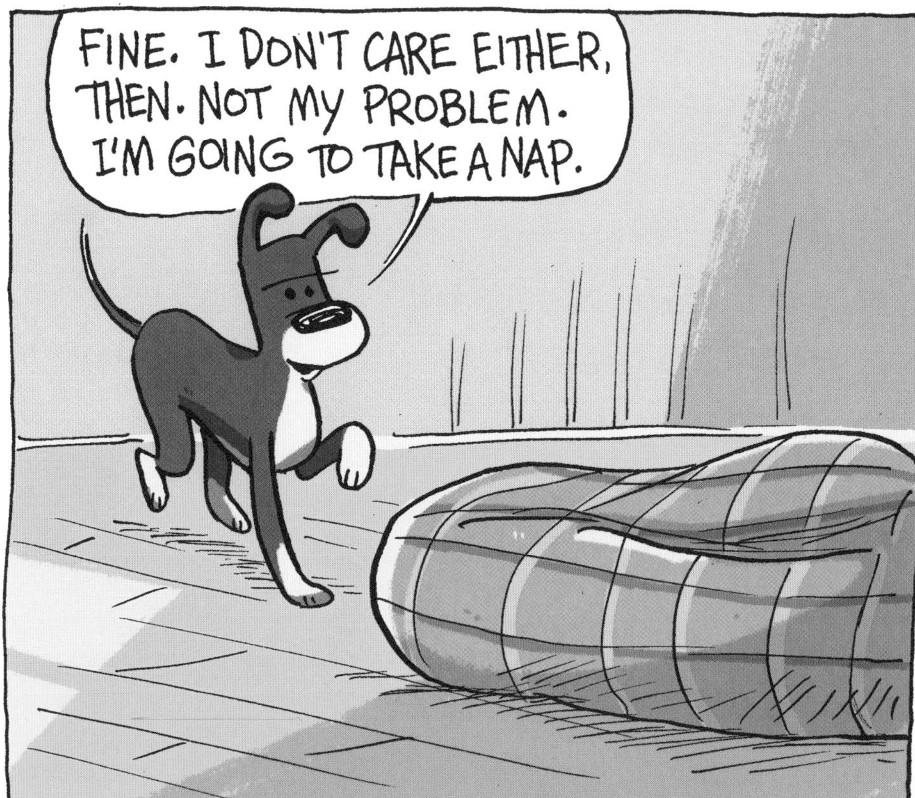
FINE. I DON'T CARE EITHER, THEN. NOT MY PROBLEM. I'M GOING TO TAKE A NAP.

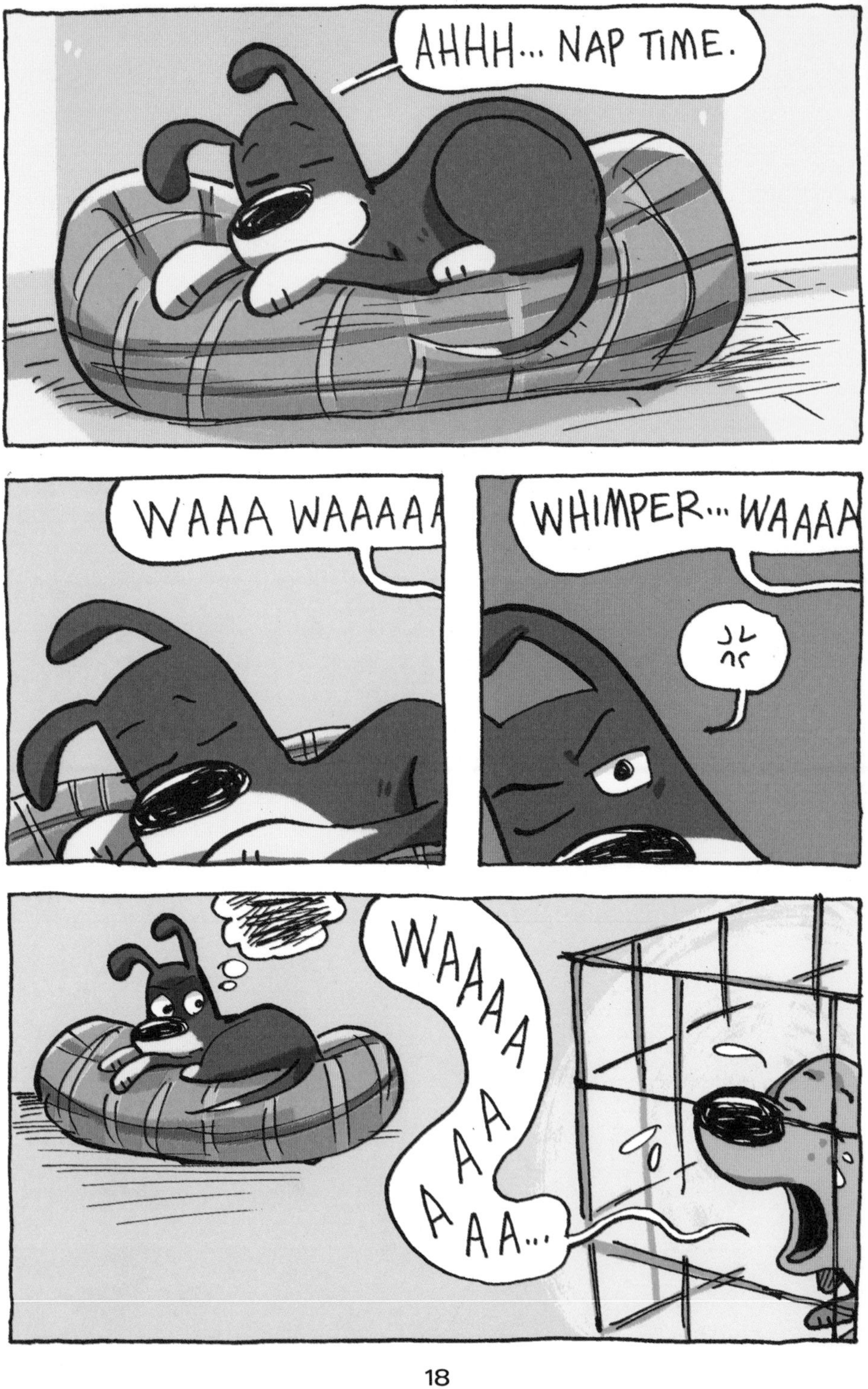
AHHH... NAP TIME.
WAAA WAAAAA
WHIMPER... WAAAA
WAAAAAAAAA...

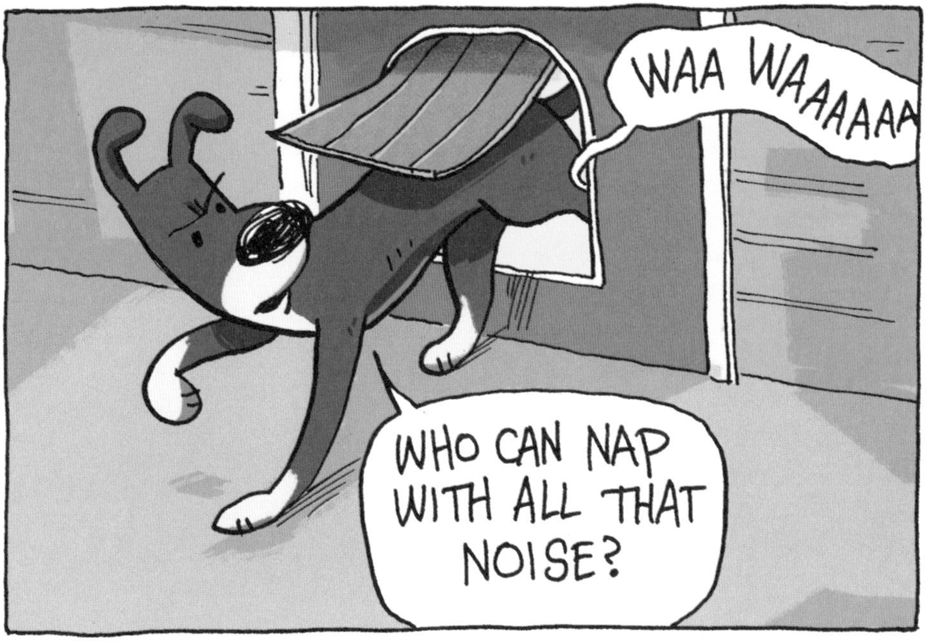
WAA WAAAAAA
WHO CAN NAP WITH ALL THAT NOISE?
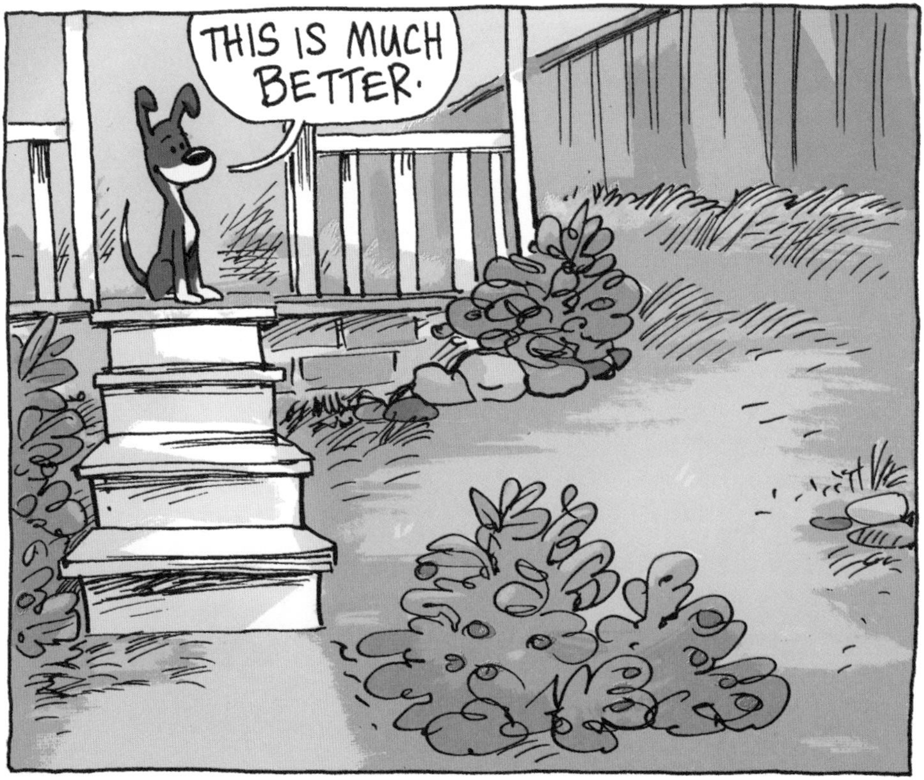
THIS IS MUCH BETTER.

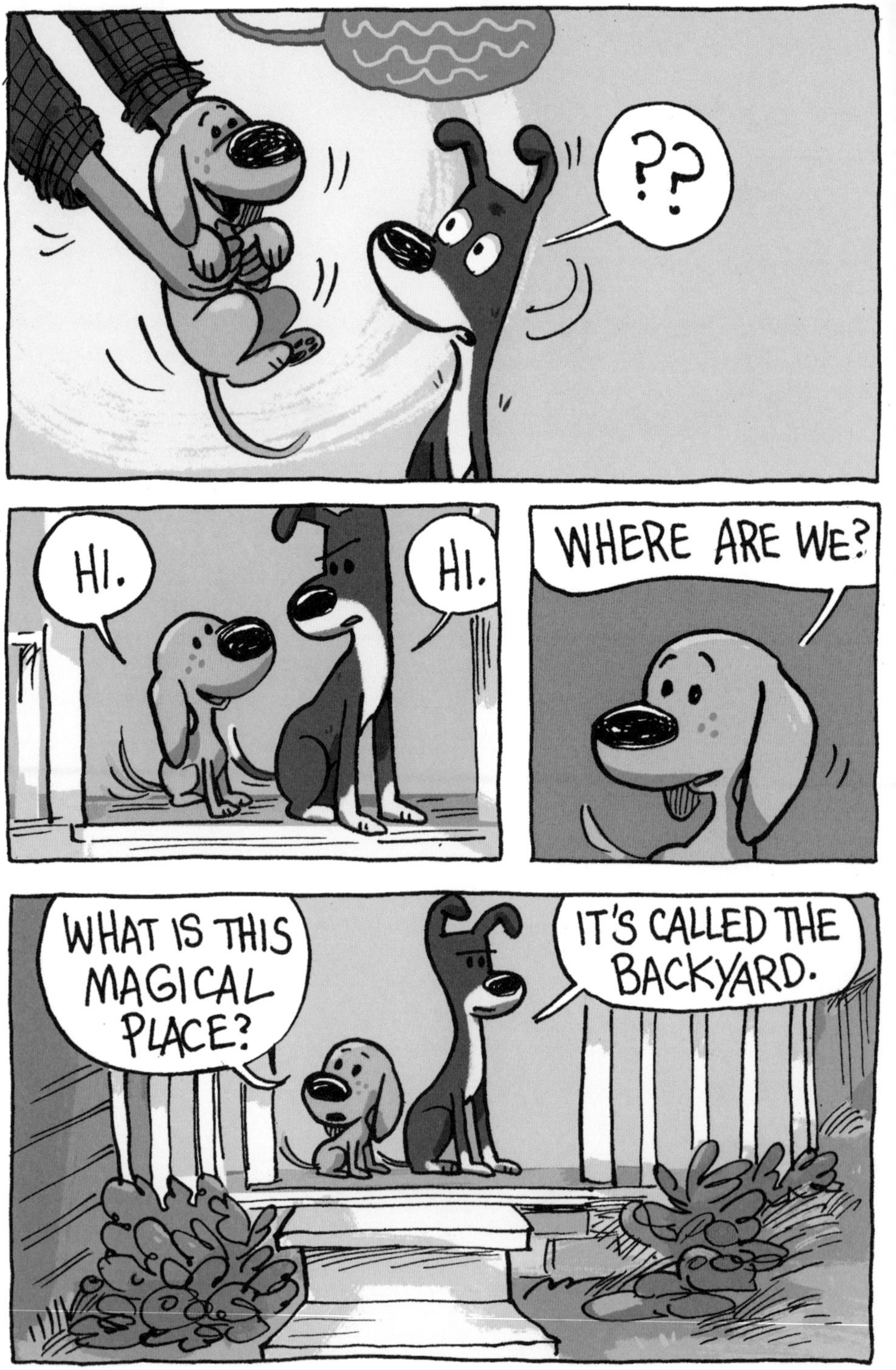
??
HI.
HI.
WHERE ARE WE?
WHAT IS THIS MAGICAL PLACE?
IT'S CALLED THE BACKYARD.

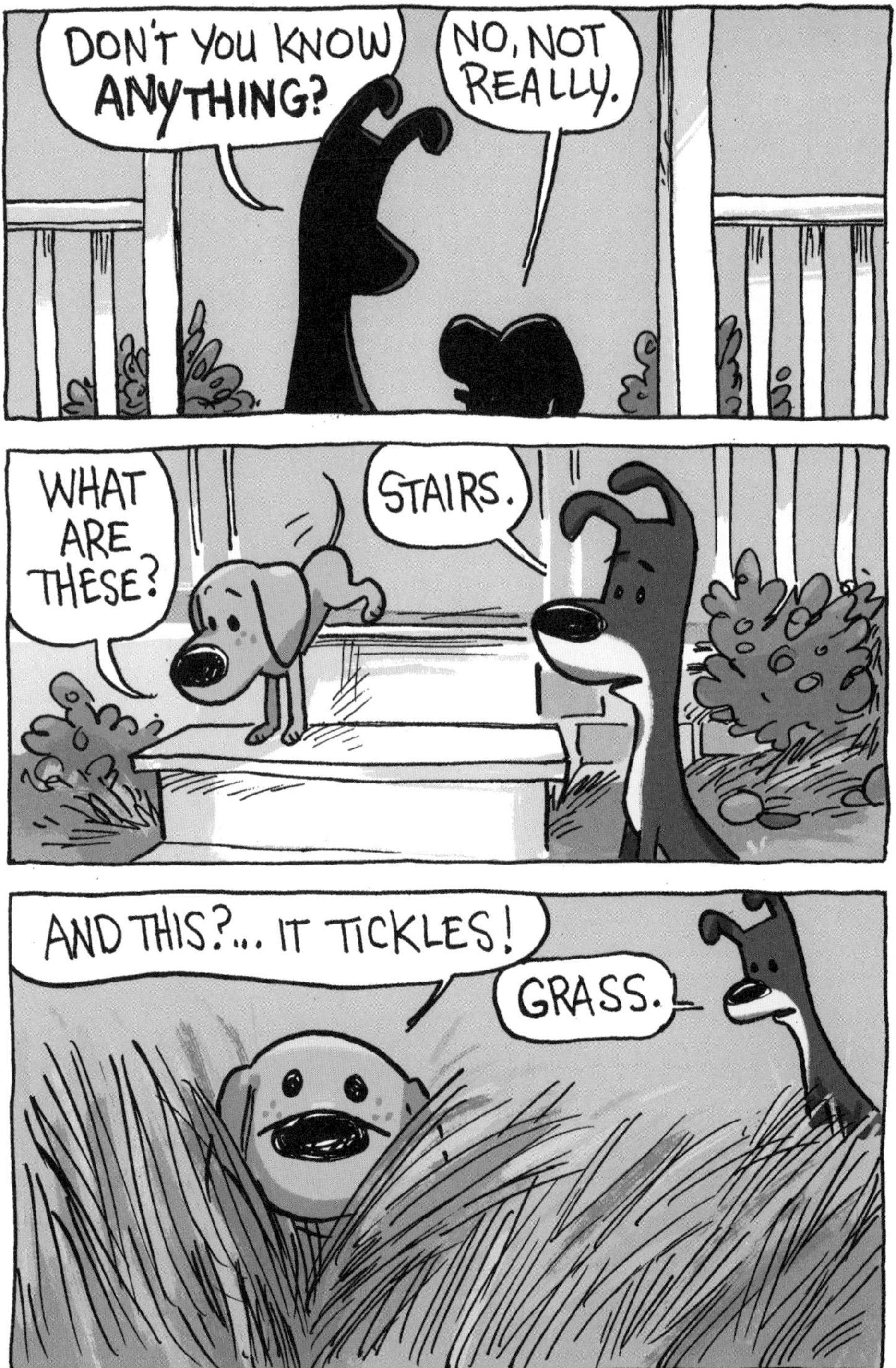
DON'T YOU KNOW ANYTHING?
NO, NOT REALLY.
WHAT ARE THESE?
STAIRS.
AND THIS?... IT TICKLES!
GRASS.

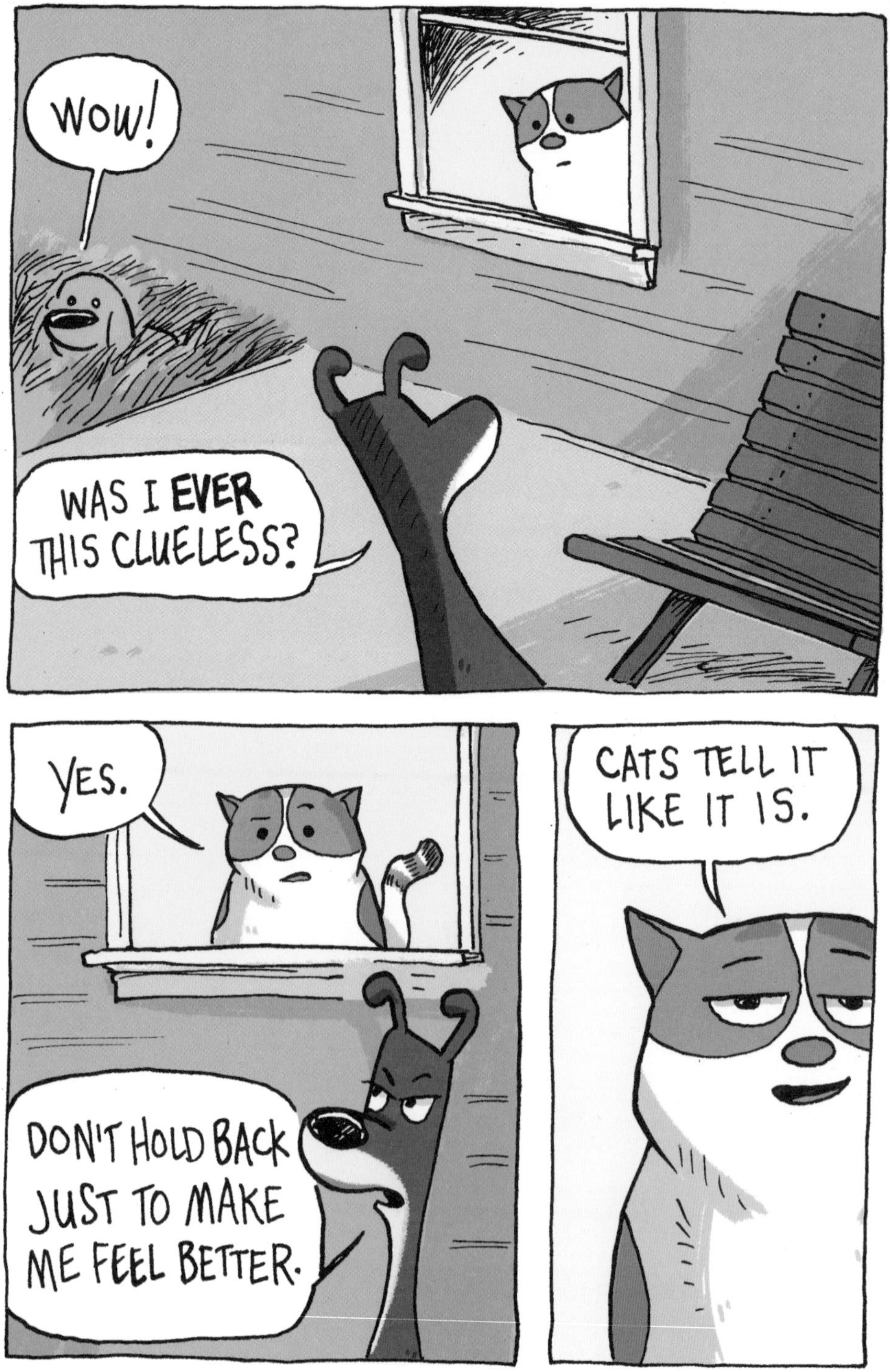
WOW!
WAS I **EVER** THIS CLUELESS?
YES.
DON'T HOLD BACK JUST TO MAKE ME FEEL BETTER.
CATS TELL IT LIKE IT IS.

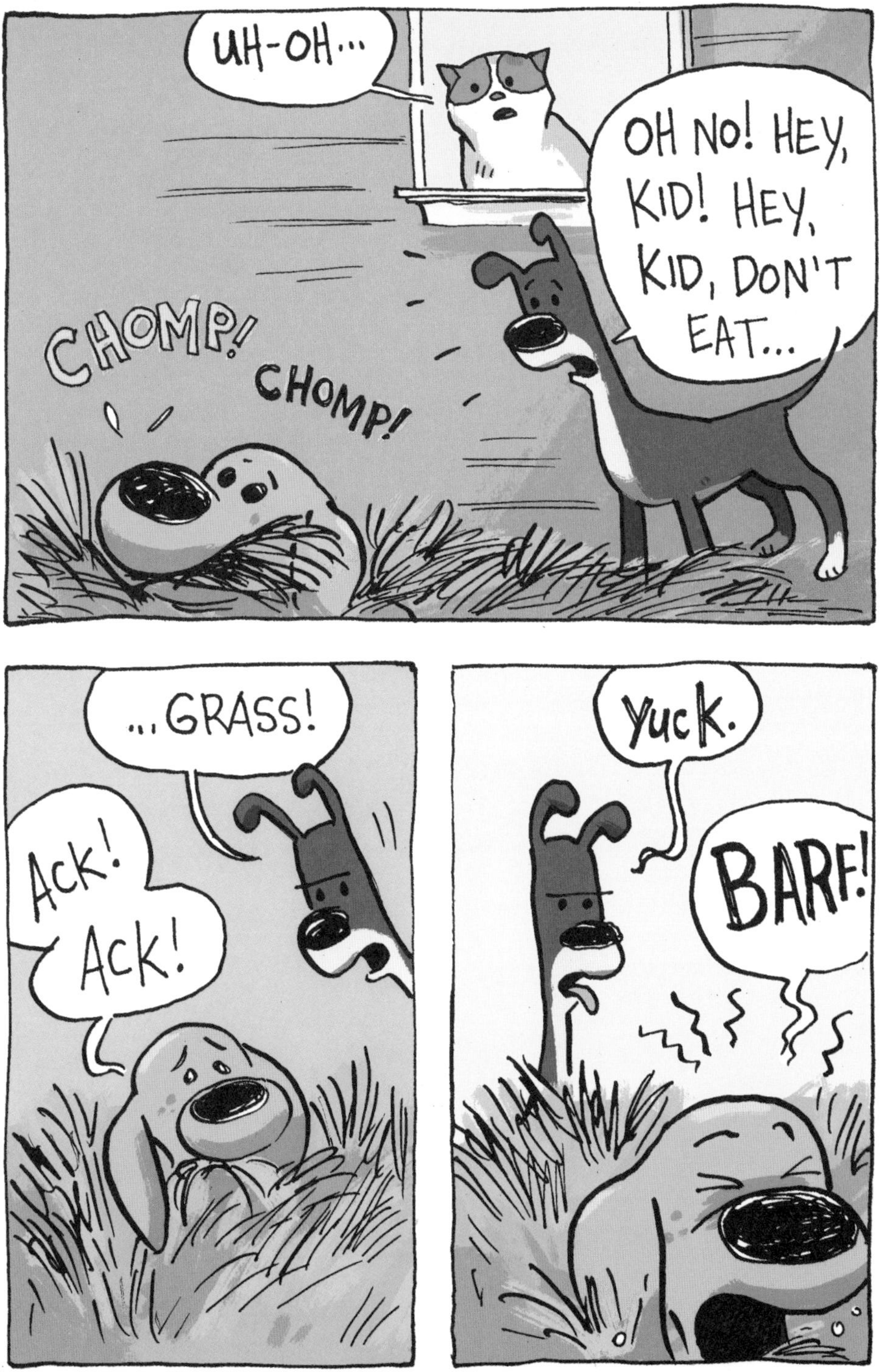
UH-OH...
OH NO! HEY, KID! HEY, KID, DON'T EAT...
CHOMP!
CHOMP!
...GRASS!
Ack! Ack!
yuck.
BARF!

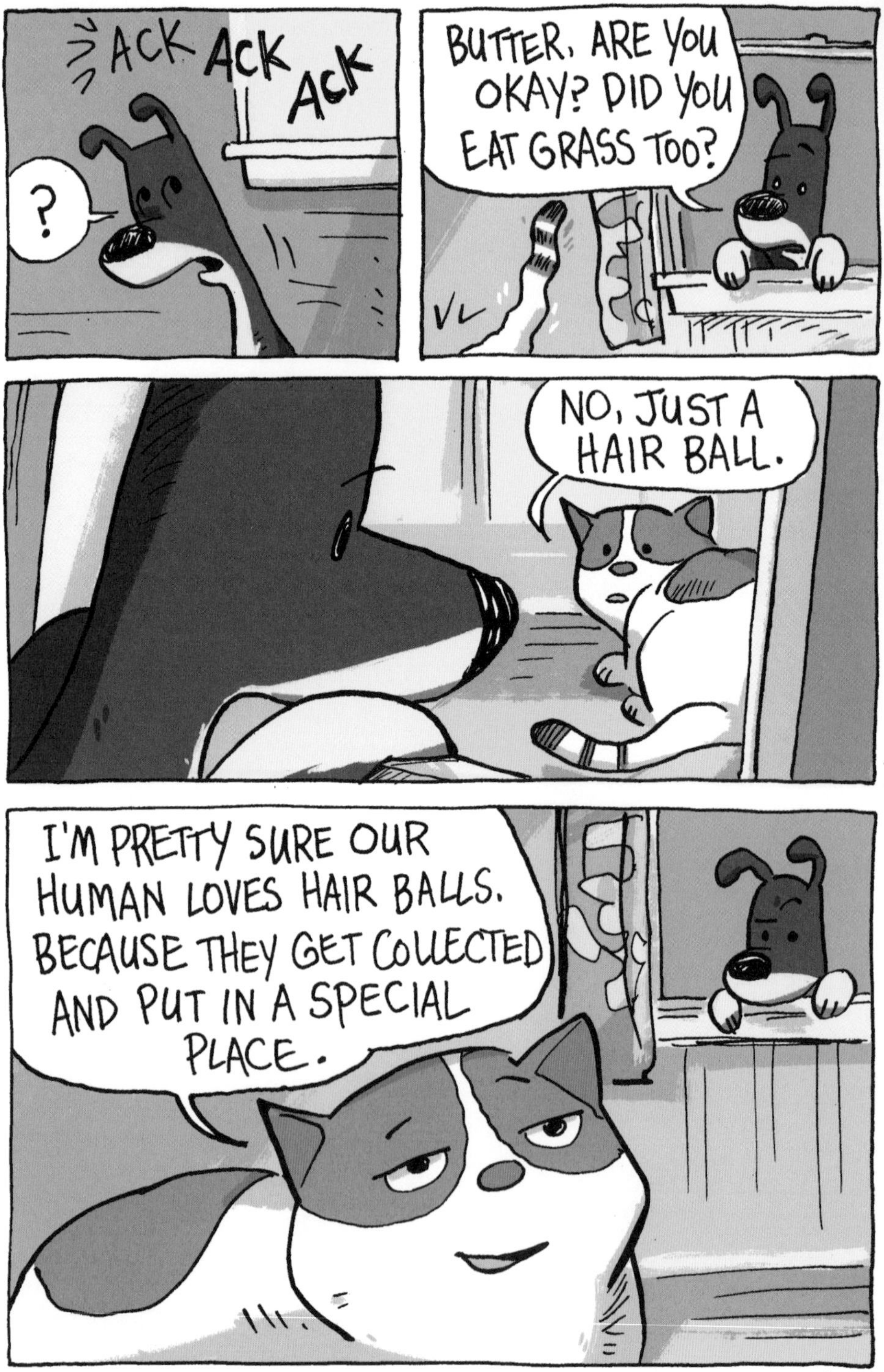
ACK ACK ACK
?
BUTTER, ARE YOU OKAY? DID YOU EAT GRASS TOO?
NO, JUST A HAIR BALL.
I'M PRETTY SURE OUR HUMAN LOVES HAIR BALLS. BECAUSE THEY GET COLLECTED AND PUT IN A SPECIAL PLACE.

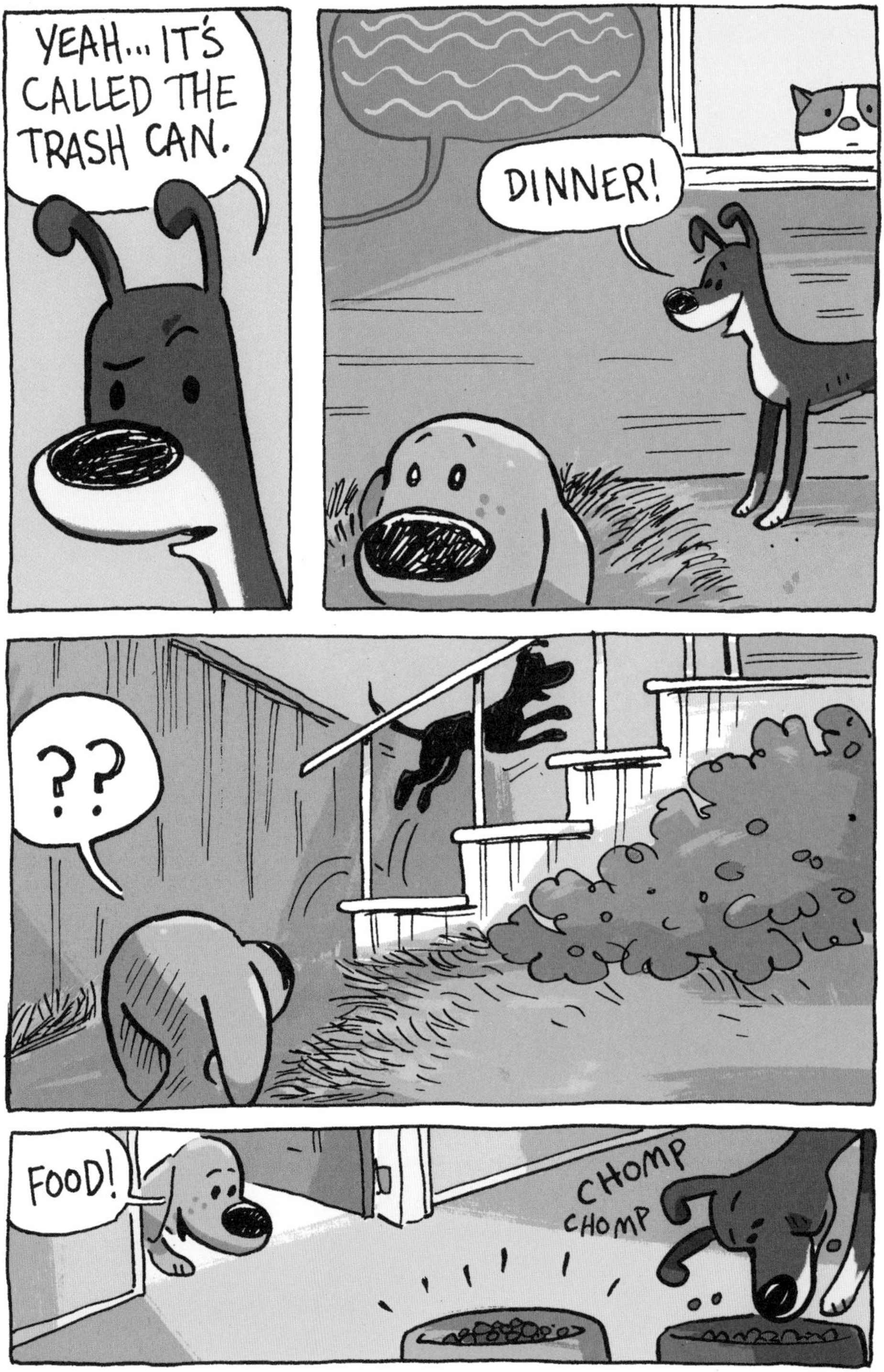
YEAH... IT'S CALLED THE TRASH CAN.
DINNER!
??
FOOD!
CHOMP
CHOMP

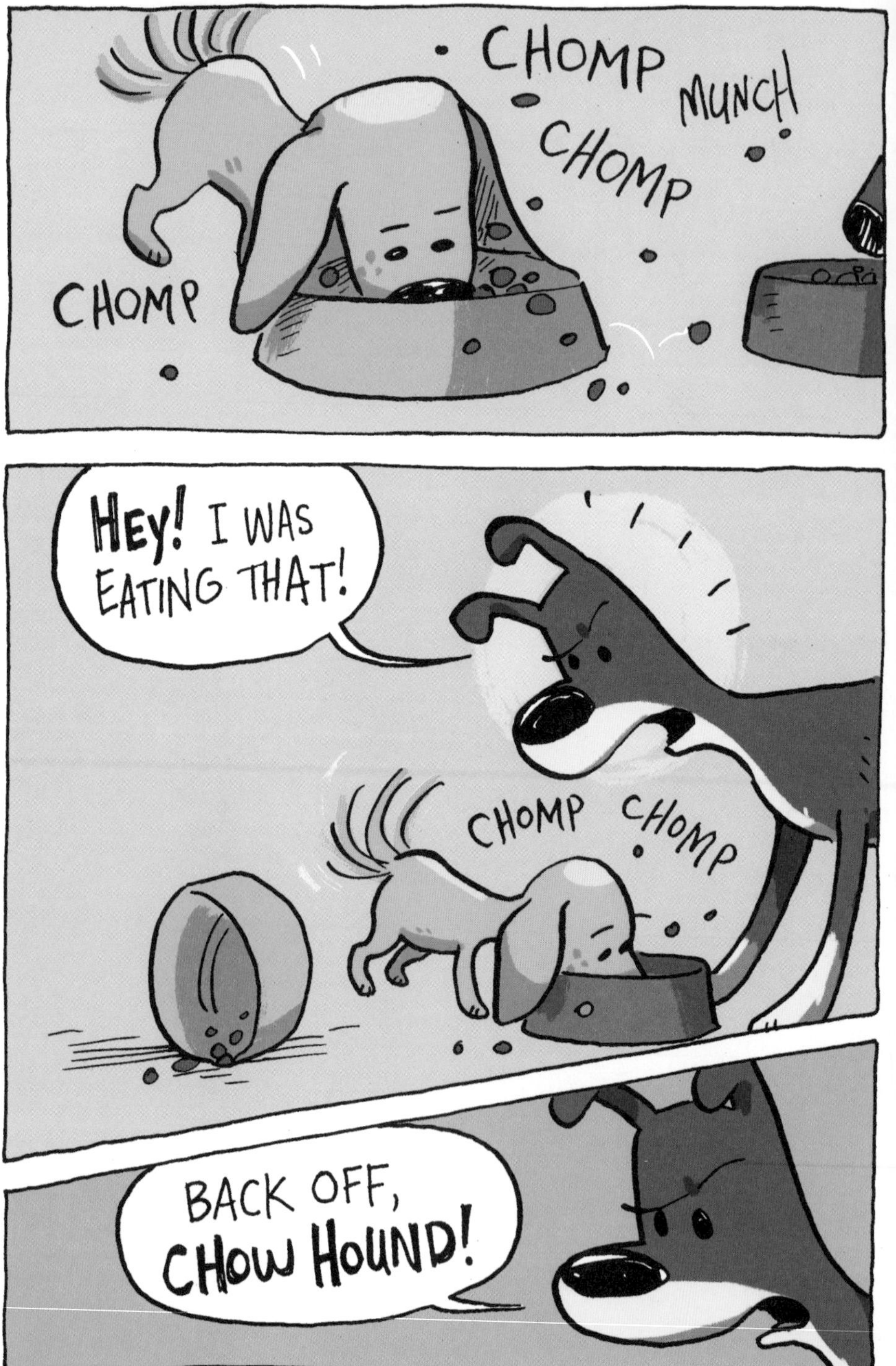
CHOMP
MUNCH
CHOMP
CHOMP
HEY! I WAS EATING THAT!
CHOMP
CHOMP
BACK OFF, CHOW HOUND!

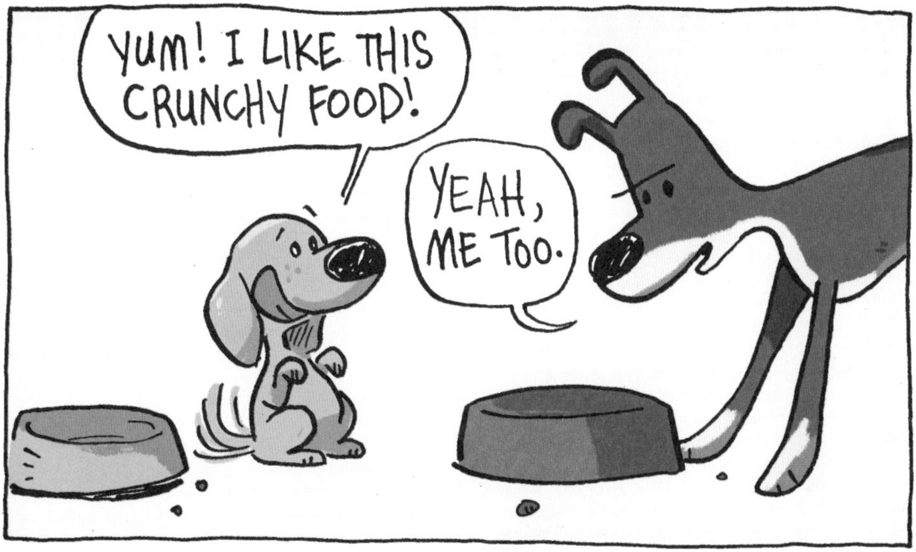
YUM! I LIKE THIS CRUNCHY FOOD!
YEAH, ME TOO.

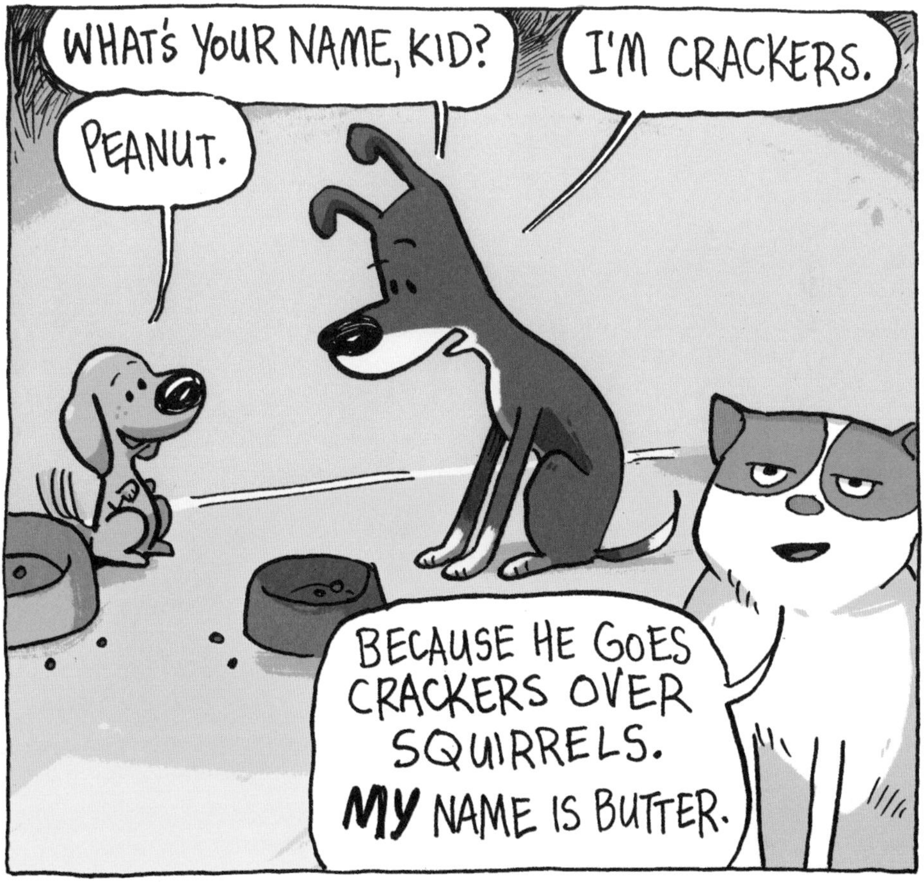
WHAT'S YOUR NAME, KID?
PEANUT.
I'M CRACKERS.
BECAUSE HE GOES CRACKERS OVER SQUIRRELS.
MY NAME IS BUTTER.

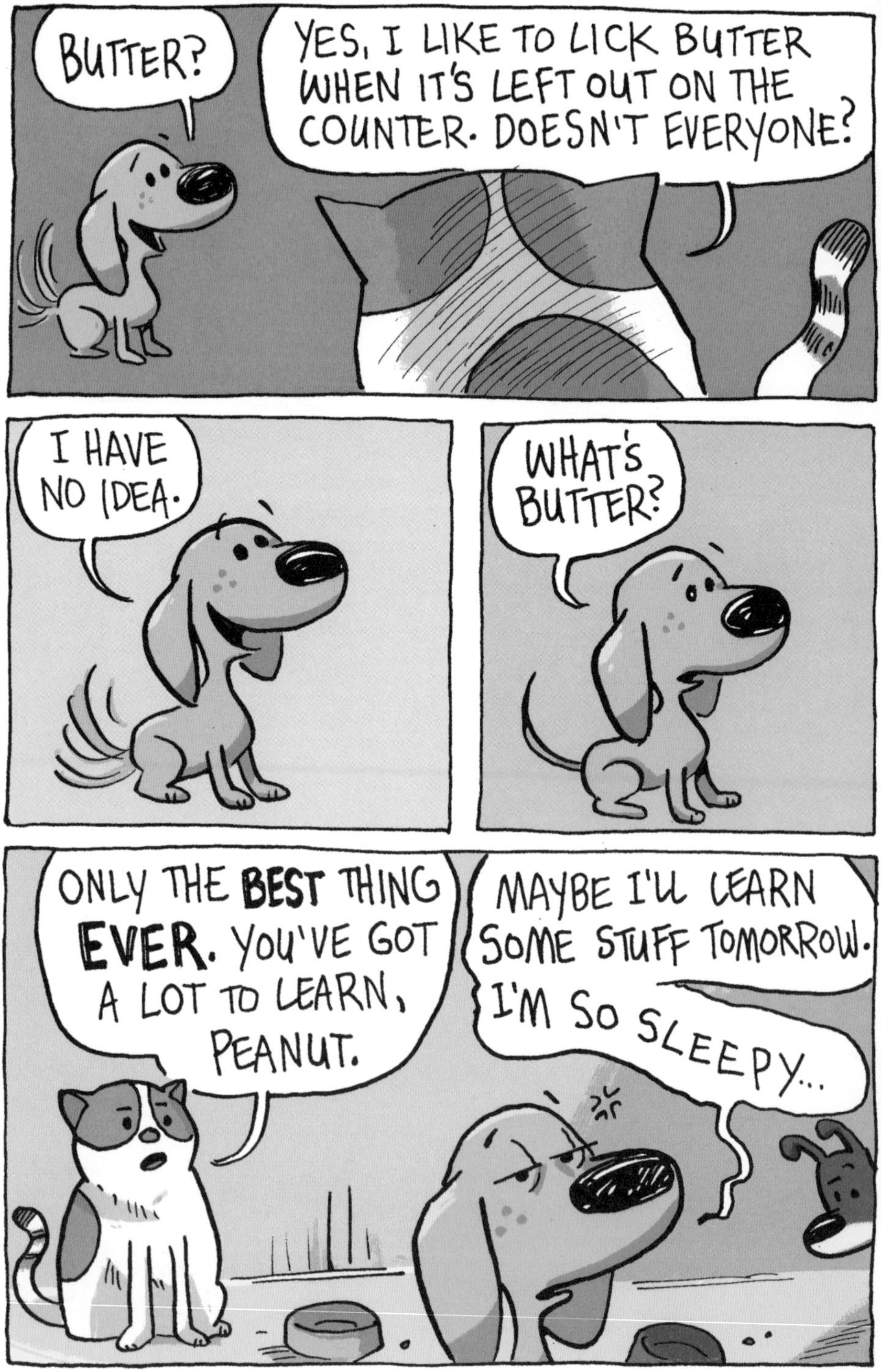
BUTTER?
YES, I LIKE TO LICK BUTTER WHEN IT'S LEFT OUT ON THE COUNTER. DOESN'T EVERYONE?
I HAVE NO IDEA.
WHAT'S BUTTER?
ONLY THE **BEST** THING **EVER**. YOU'VE GOT A LOT TO LEARN, PEANUT.
MAYBE I'LL LEARN SOME STUFF TOMORROW. I'M SO SLEEPY...

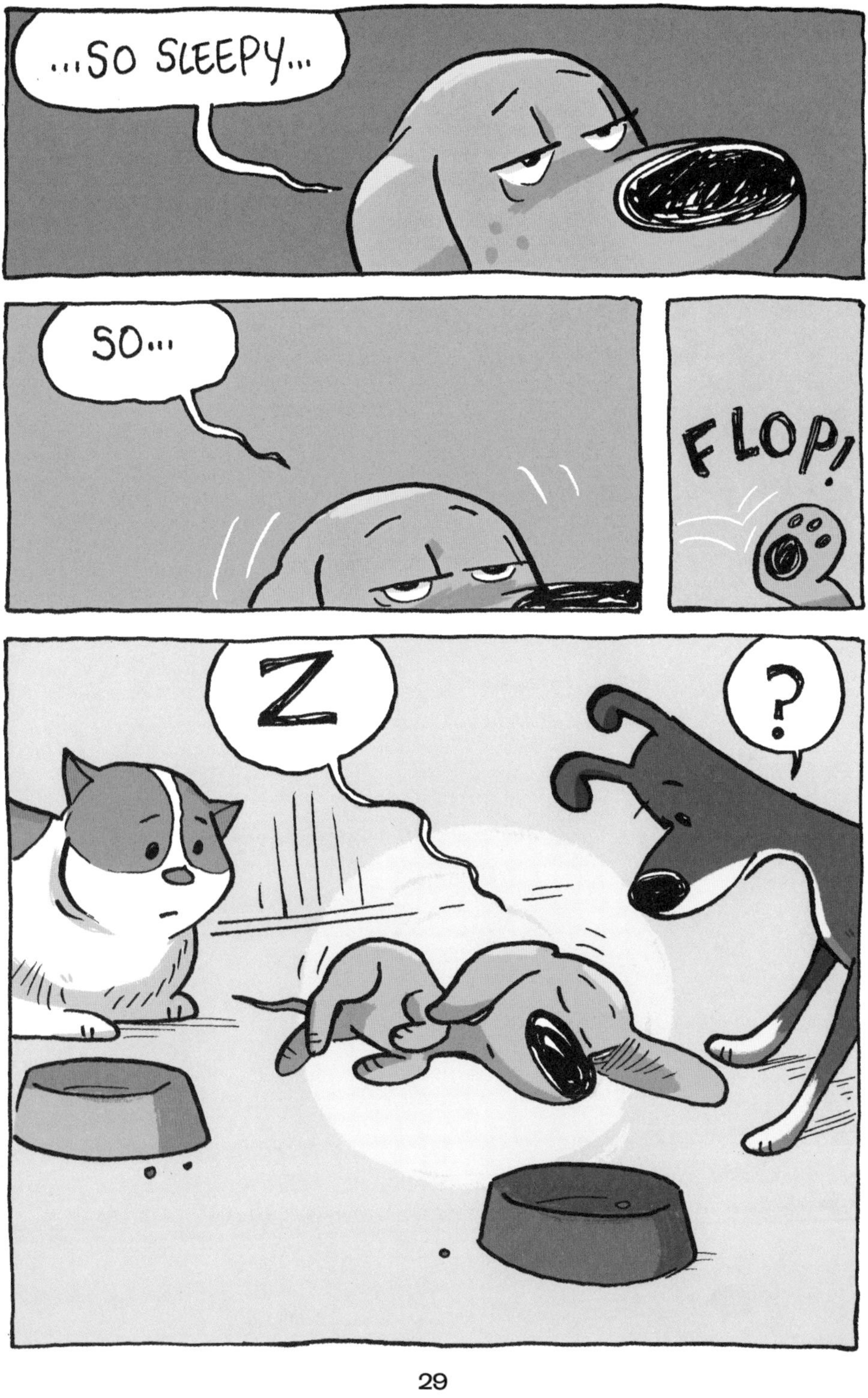
...SO SLEEPY...
SO...
FLOP!
Z
?

33

35

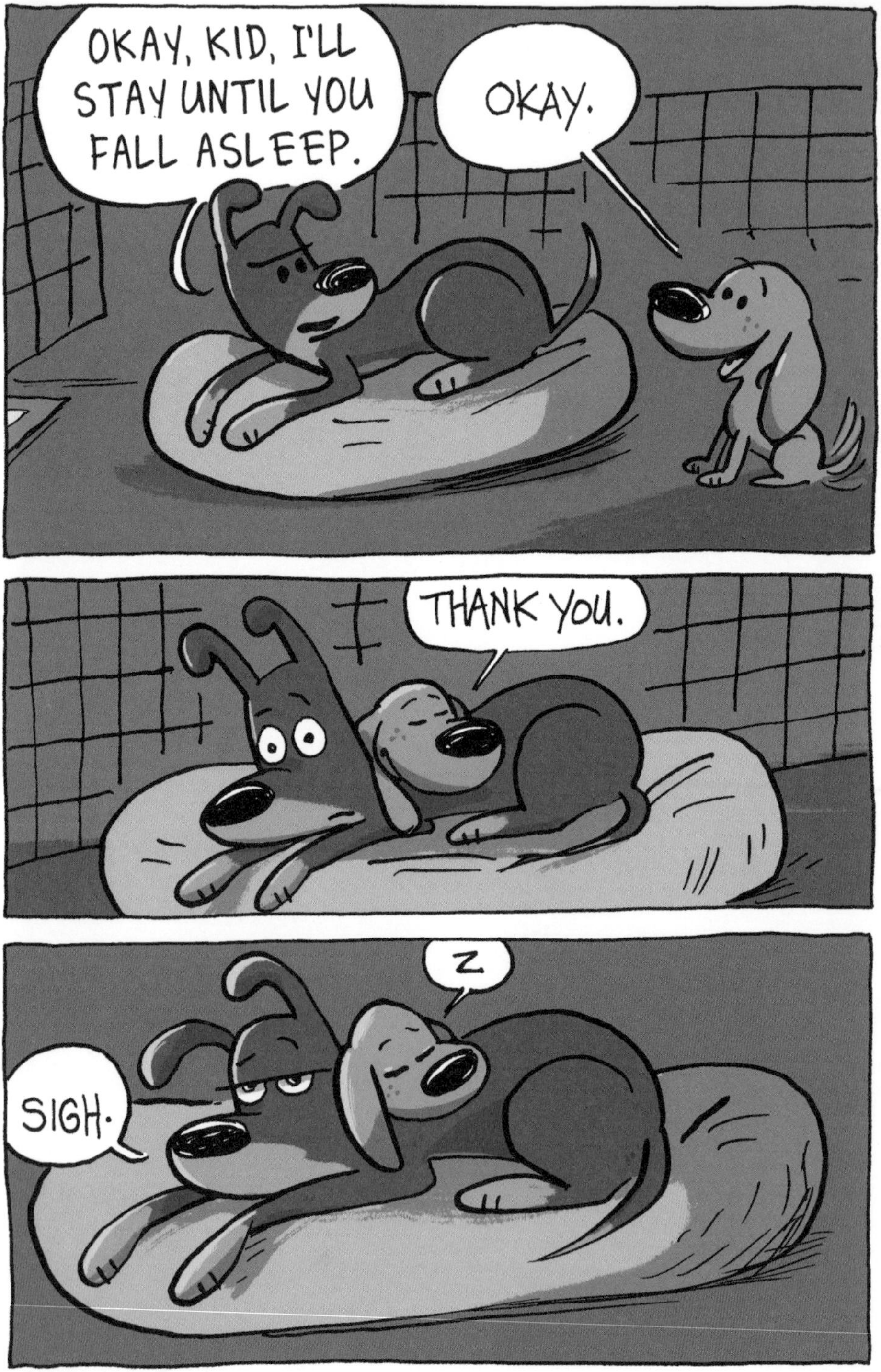
OKAY, KID, I'LL STAY UNTIL YOU FALL ASLEEP.
OKAY.
THANK YOU.
Z
SIGH.

37

39

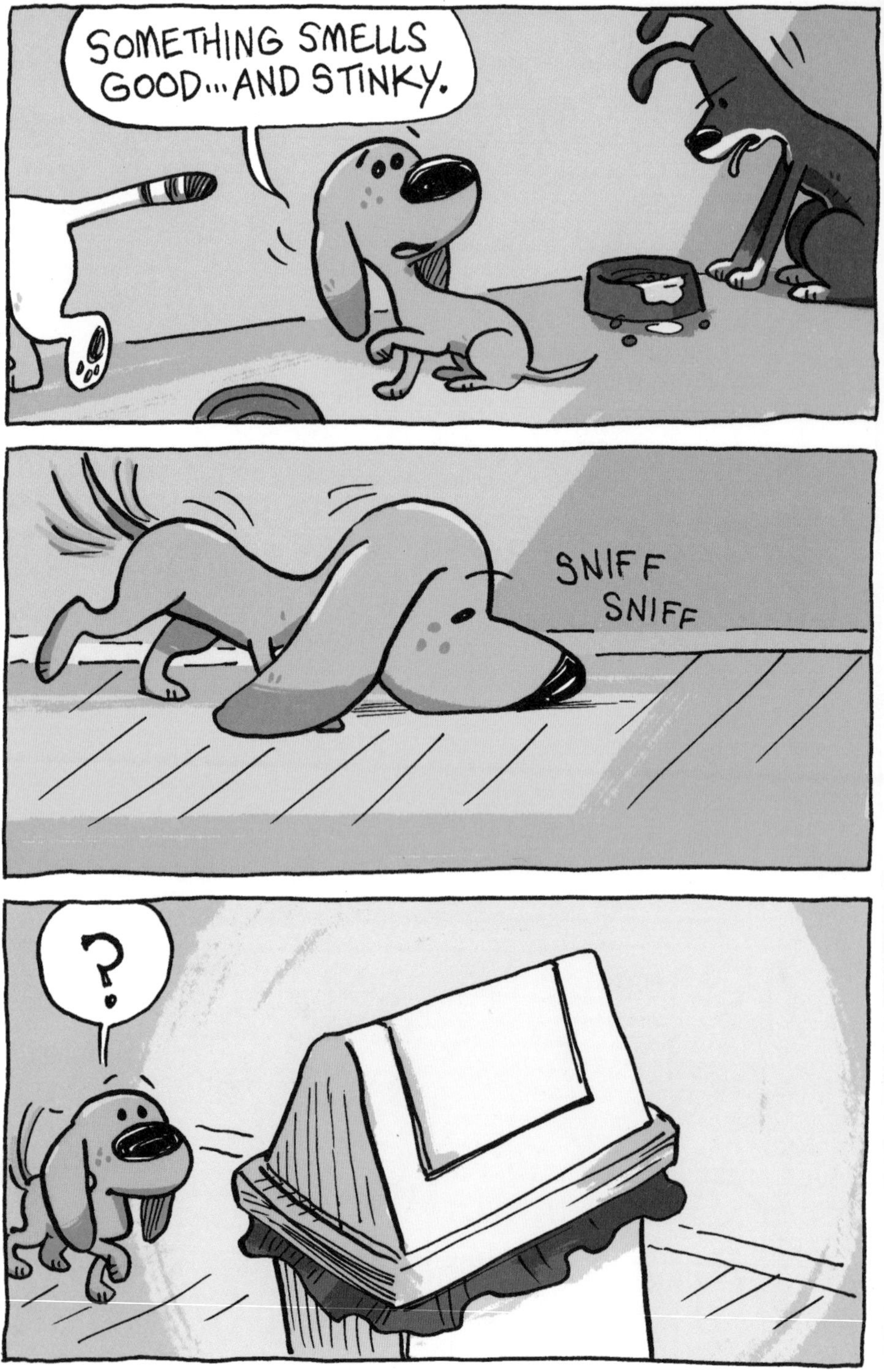
SOMETHING SMELLS GOOD... AND STINKY.
SNIFF
SNIFF
?

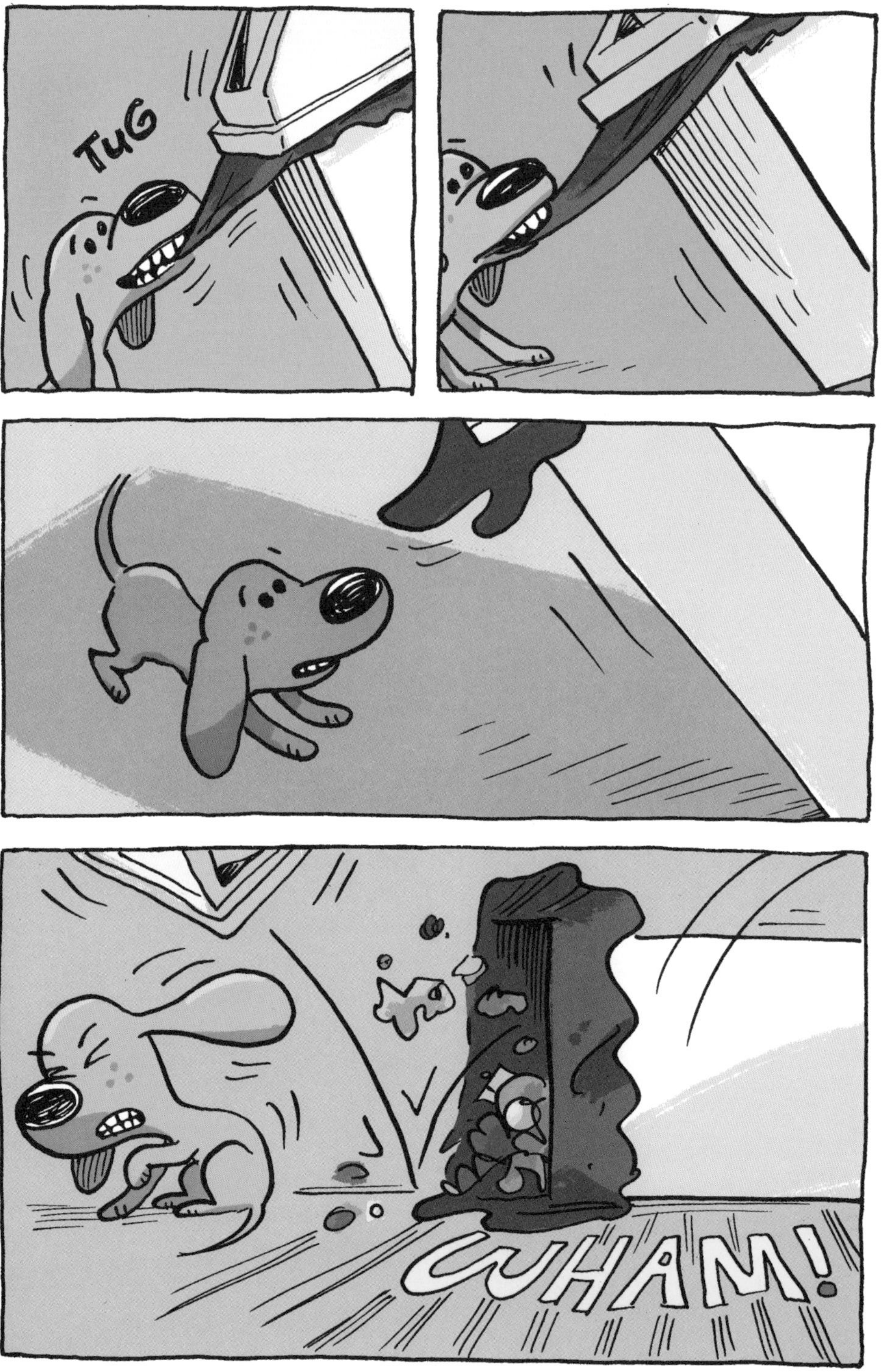
TUG
WHAM!

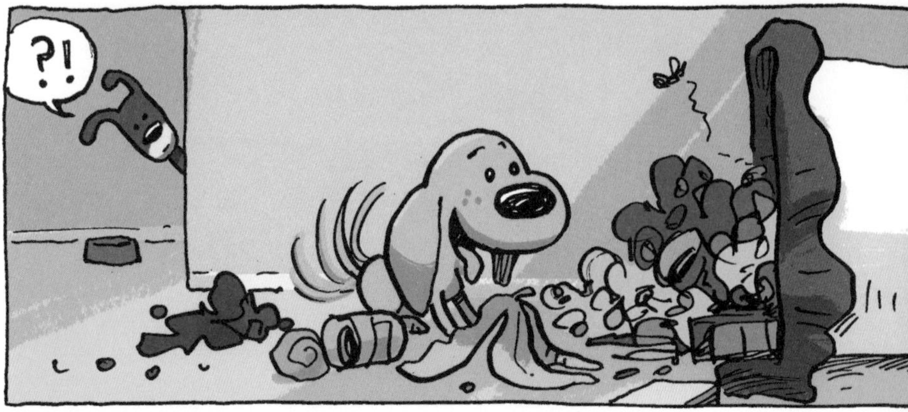
?!

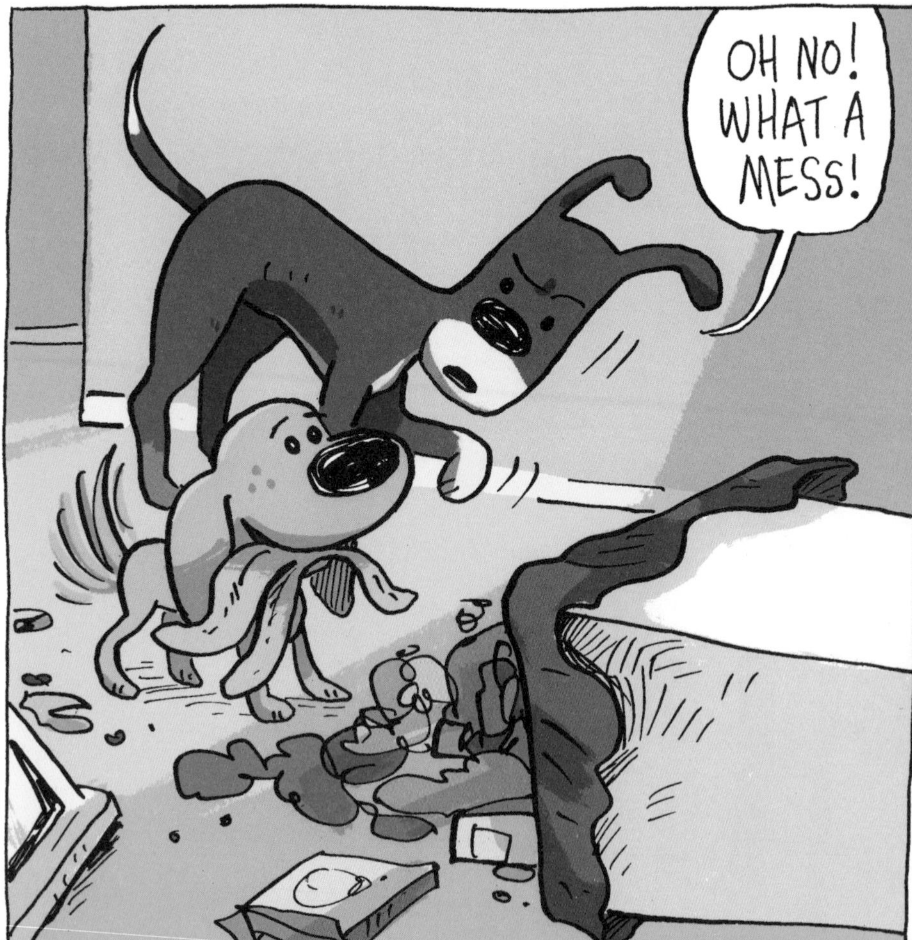
OH NO! WHAT A MESS!

43

44

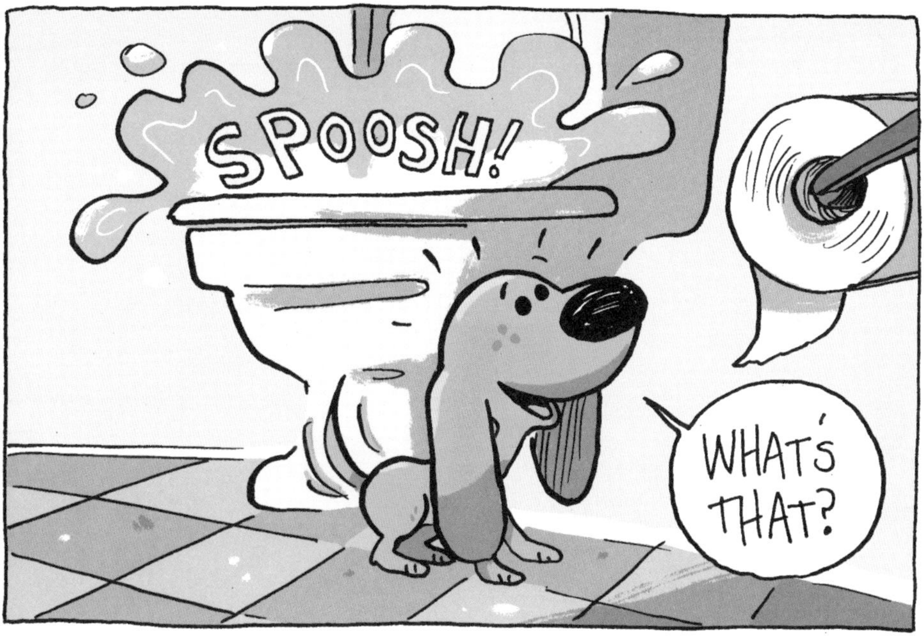
SPOOSH!
WHAT'S THAT?

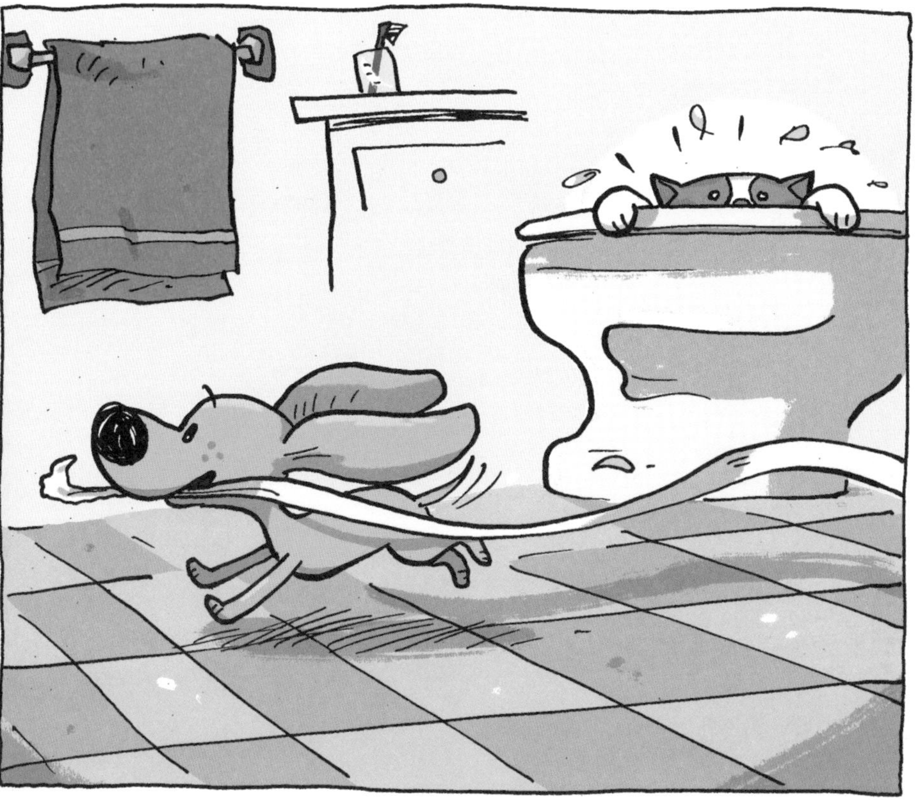

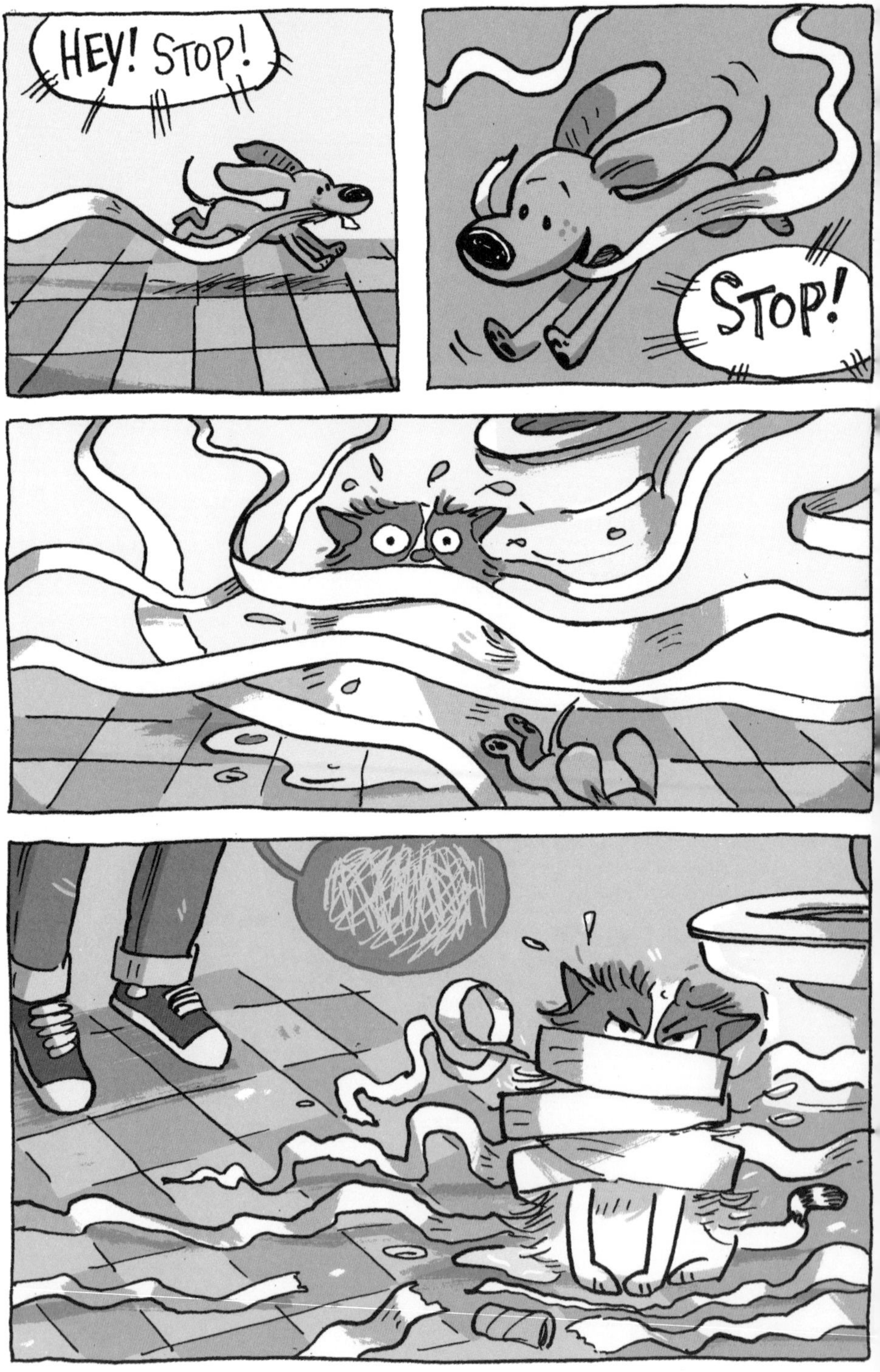
HEY! STOP!
STOP!

47

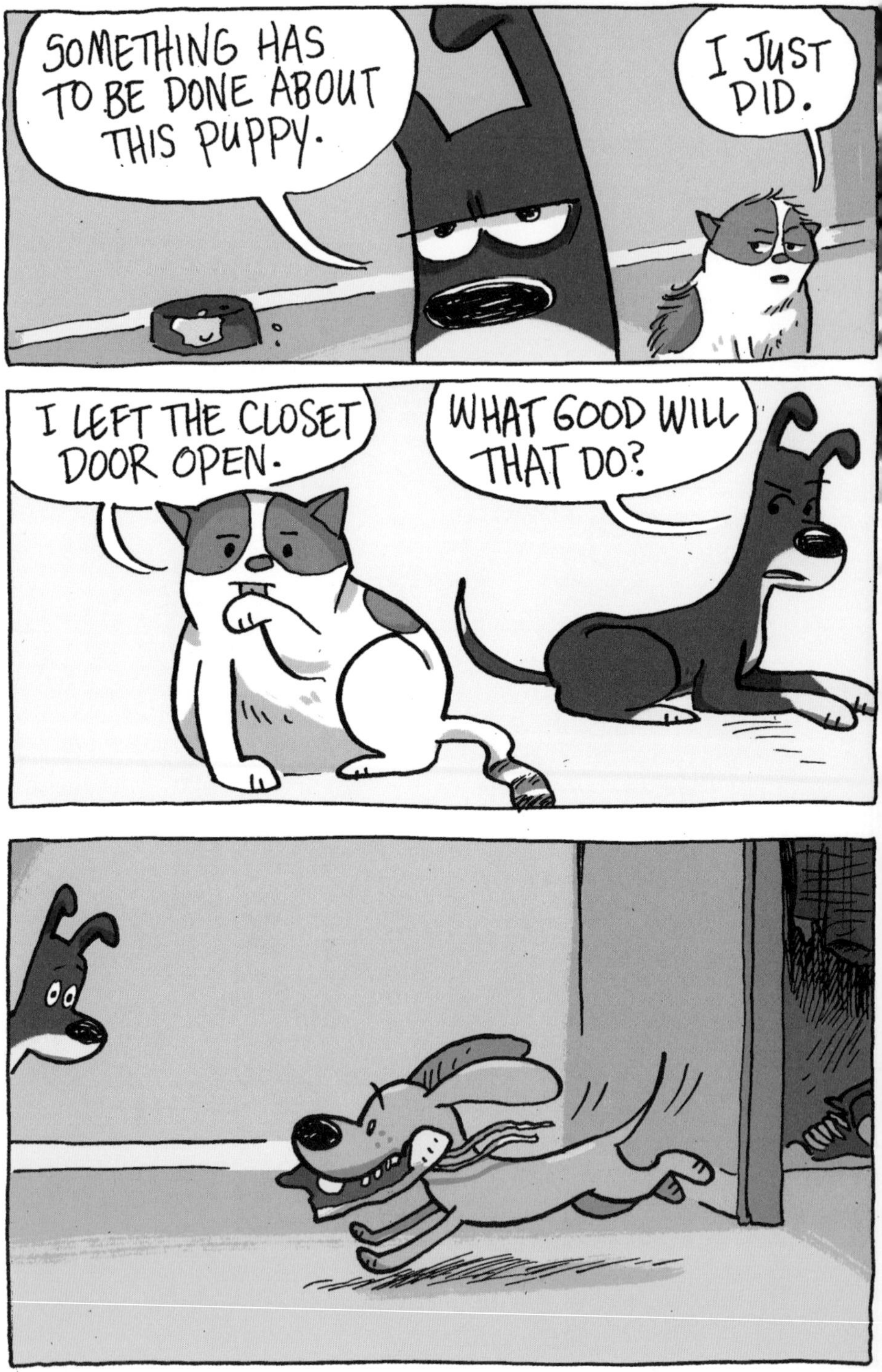
SOMETHING HAS TO BE DONE ABOUT THIS PUPPY.
I JUST DID.
I LEFT THE CLOSET DOOR OPEN.
WHAT GOOD WILL THAT DO?

49

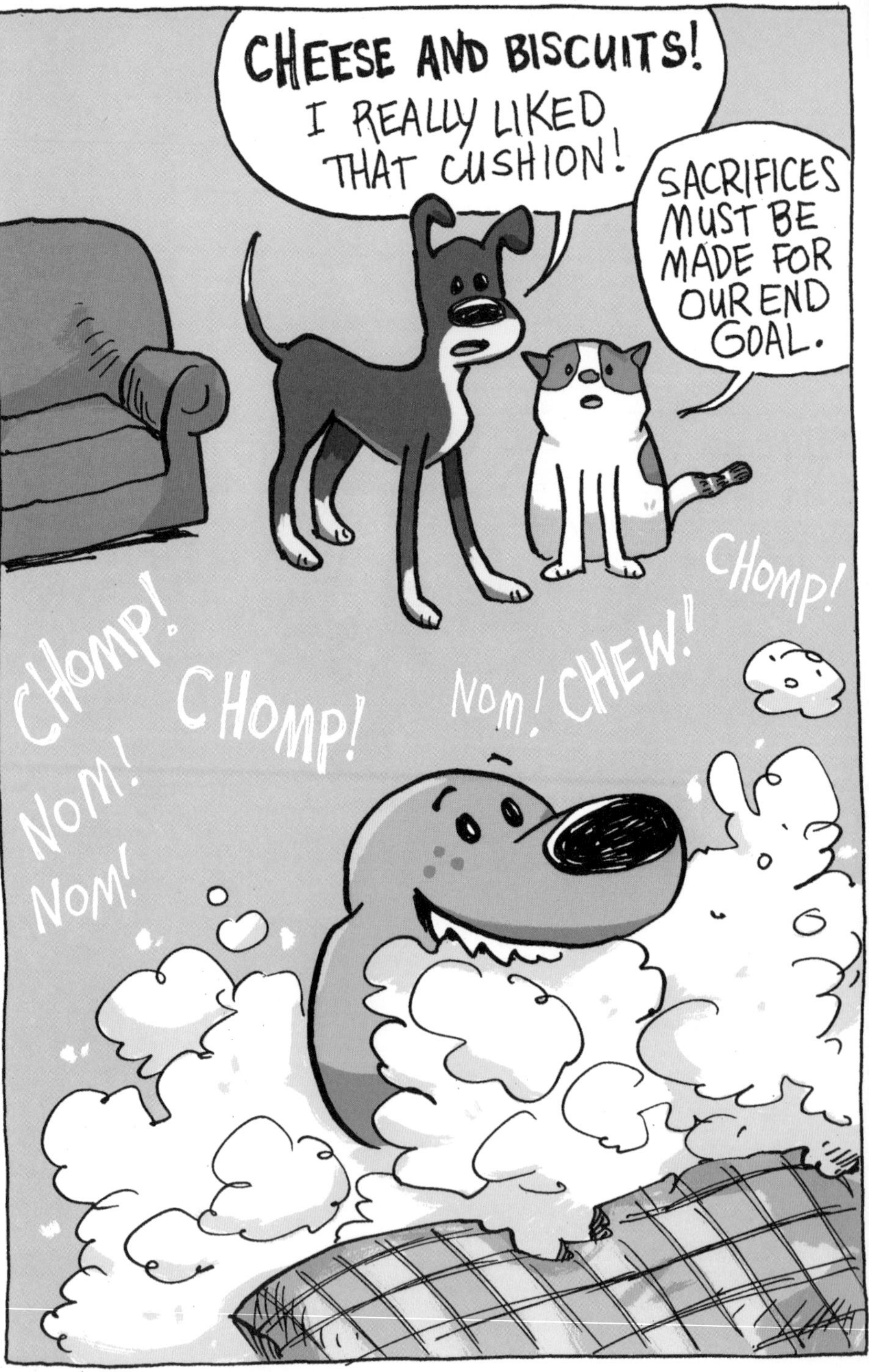
CHEESE AND BISCUITS! I REALLY LIKED THAT CUSHION!
SACRIFICES MUST BE MADE FOR OUR END GOAL.
CHOMP!
NOM!
NOM!
CHOMP!
NOM! CHEW!
CHOMP!

51

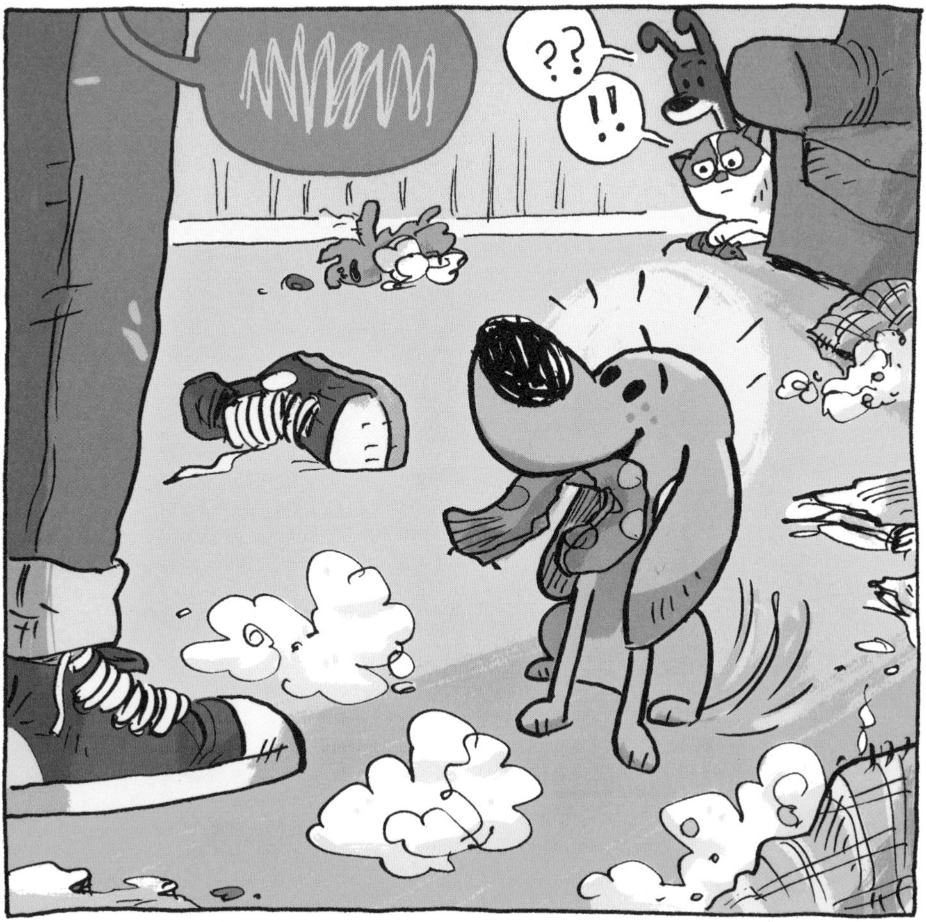
??
!!

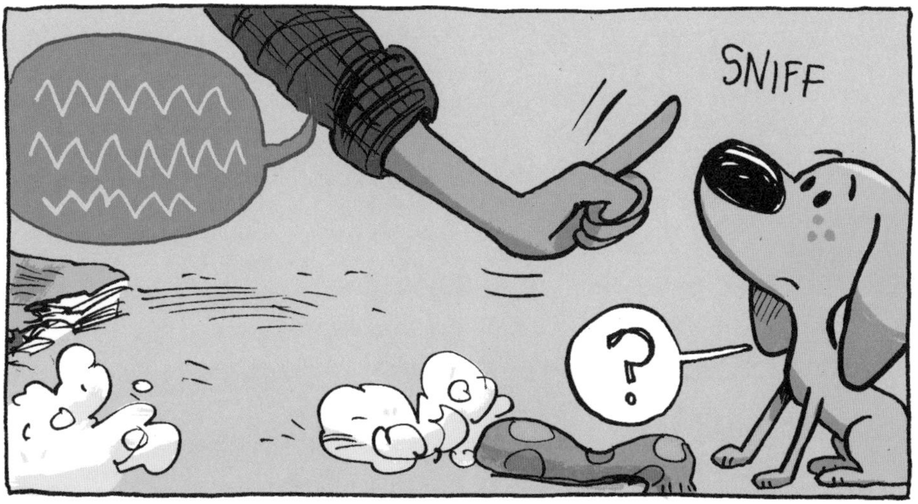
SNIFF
?

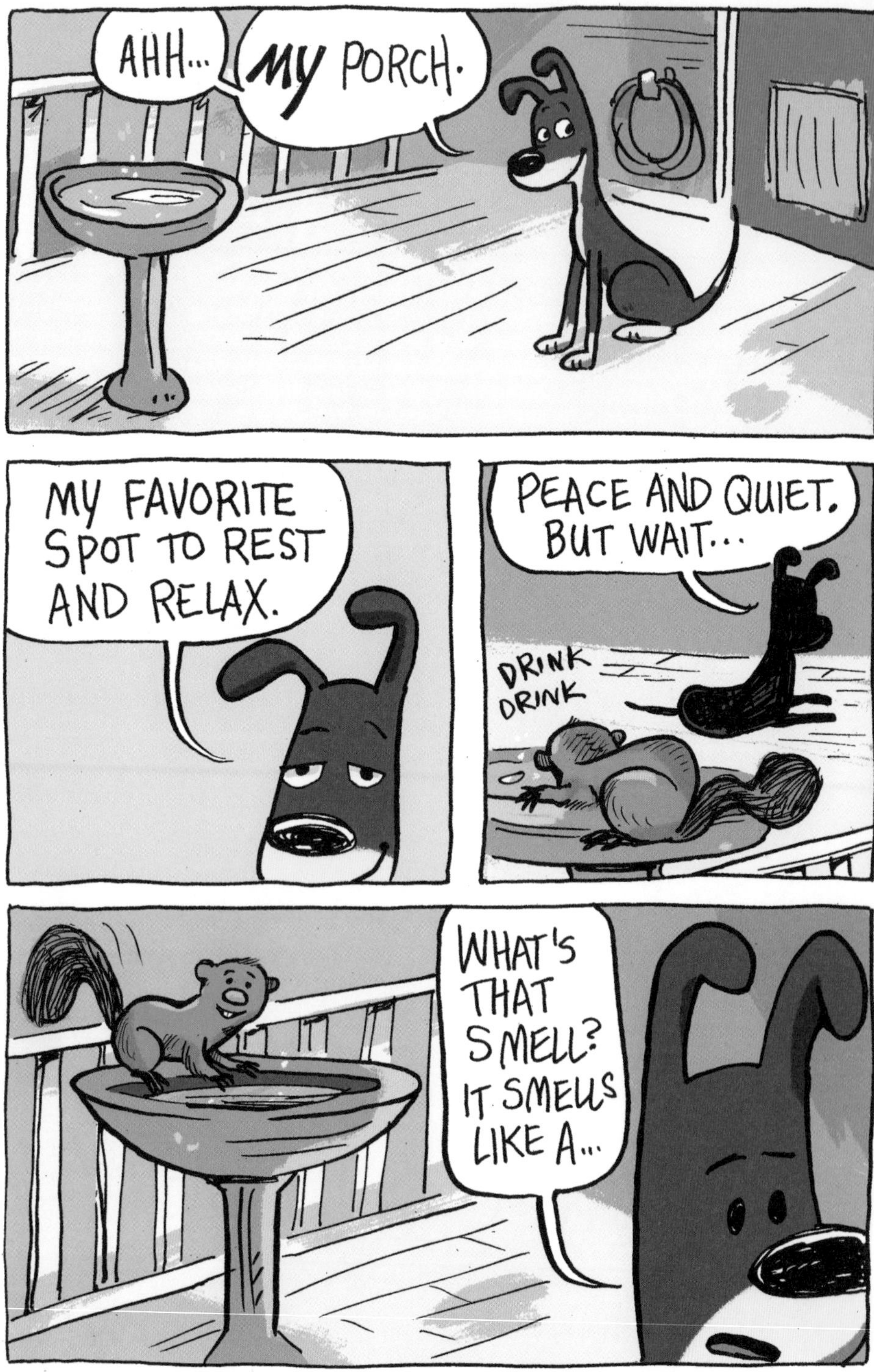
AHH...
MY PORCH.
MY FAVORITE SPOT TO REST AND RELAX.
PEACE AND QUIET. BUT WAIT...
DRINK DRINK
WHAT'S THAT SMELL? IT SMELLS LIKE A...

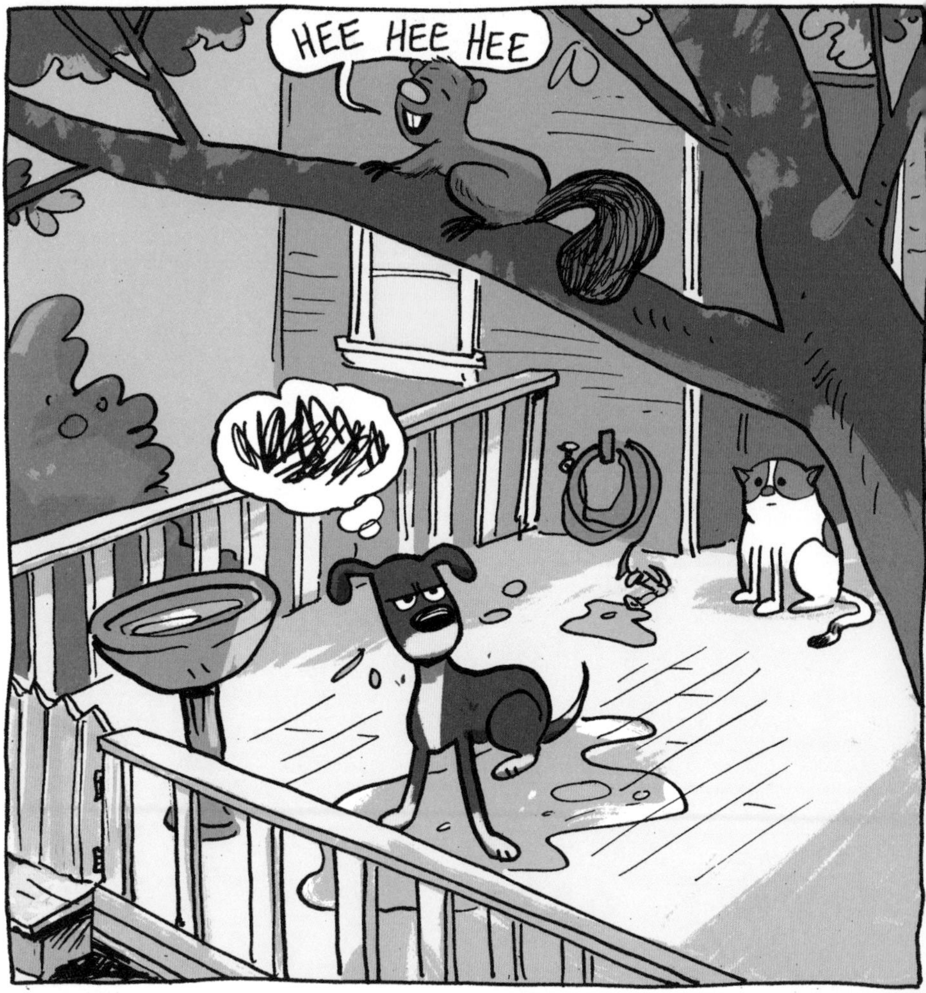
HEE HEE HEE

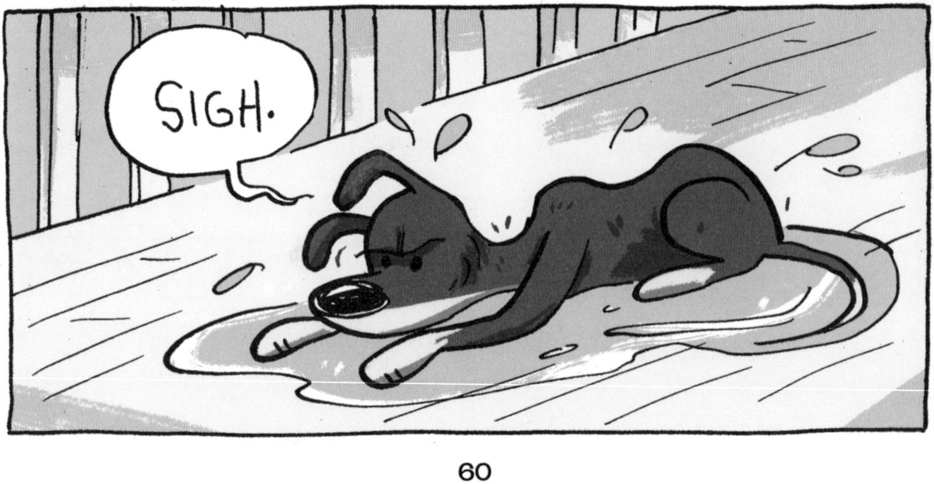
SIGH.

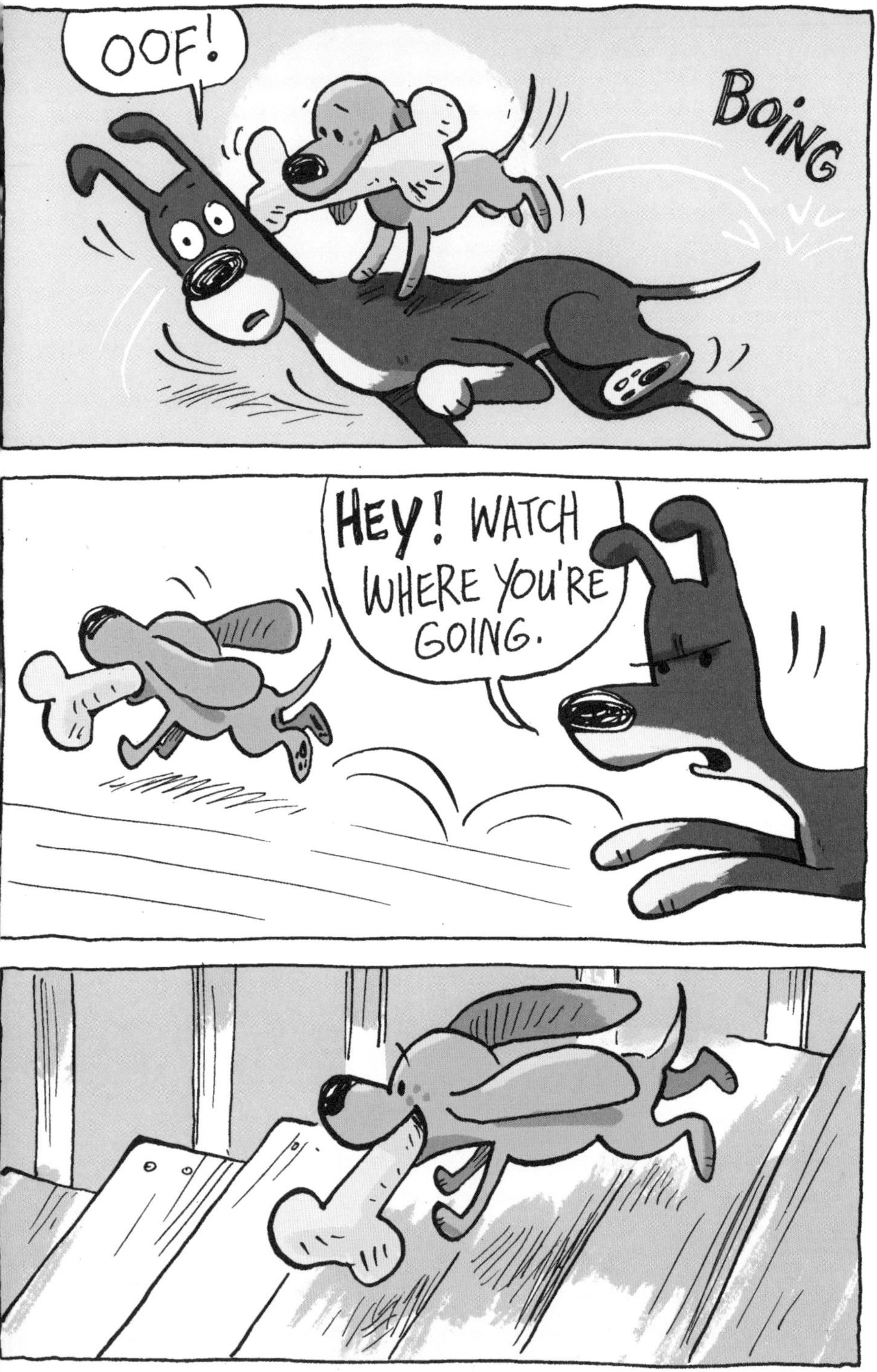
OOF!
BOING
HEY! WATCH WHERE YOU'RE GOING.

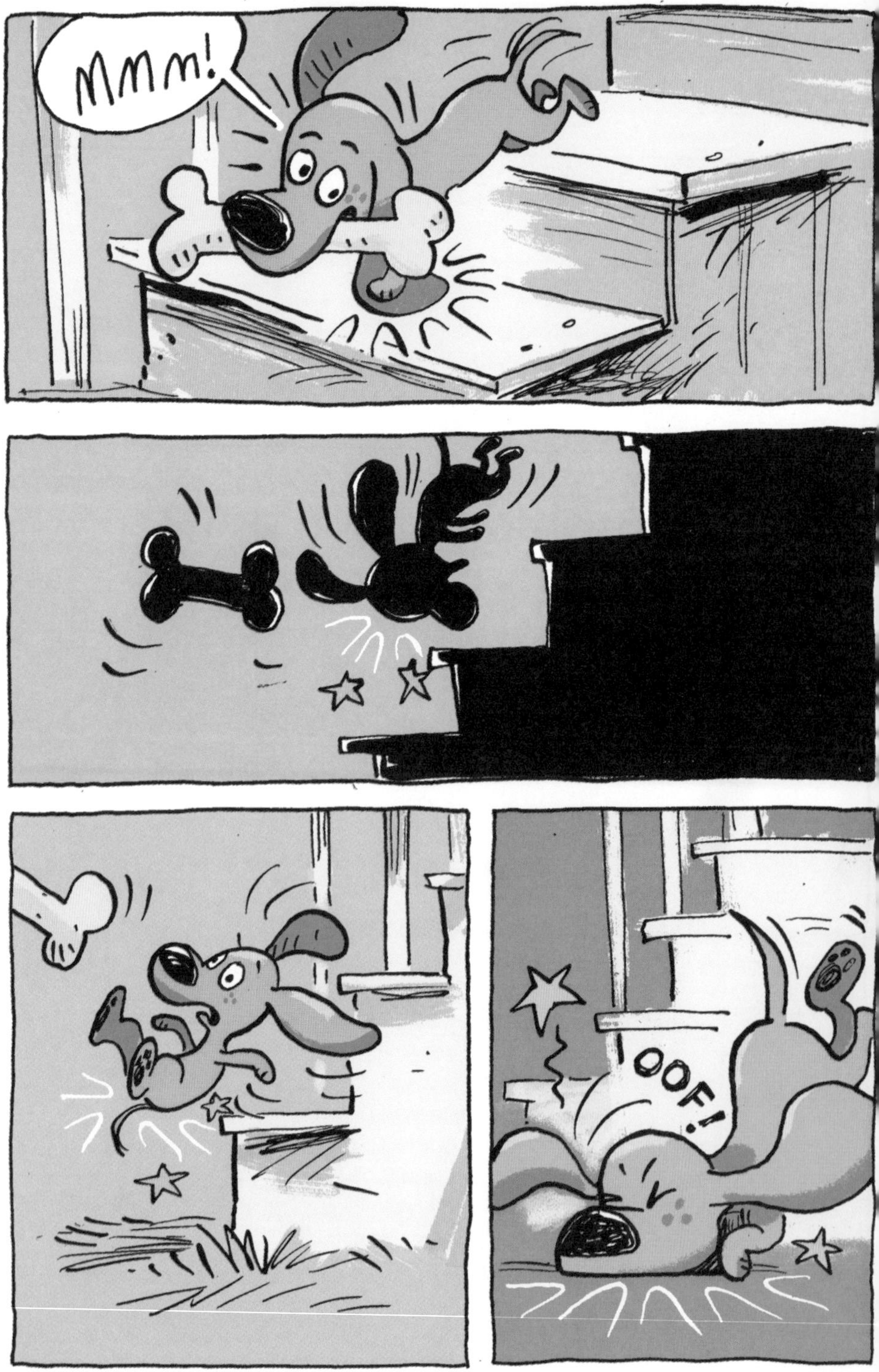
Mmm!
OOF!

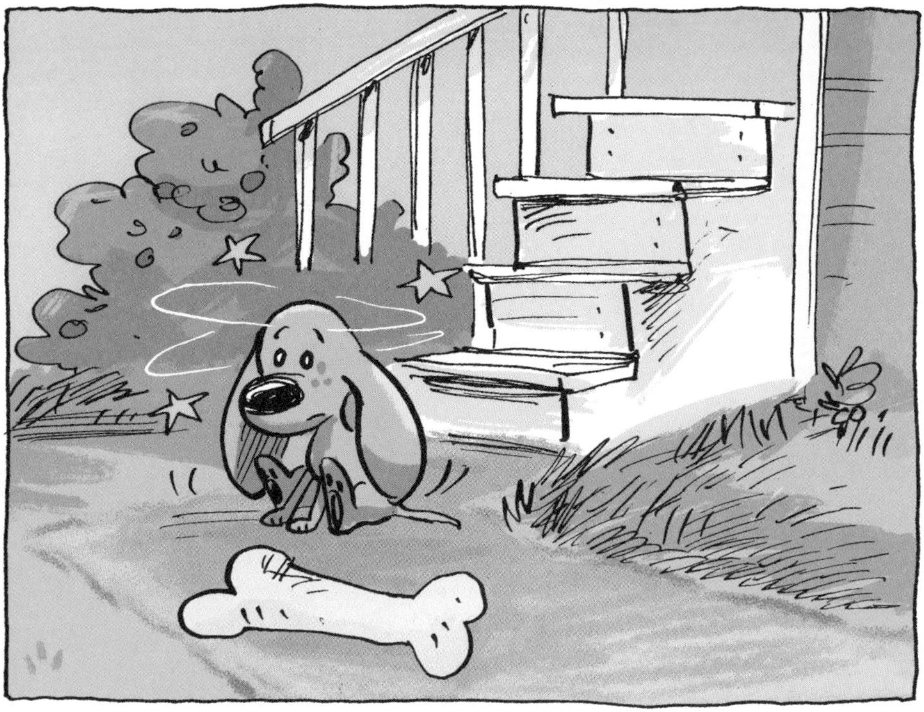

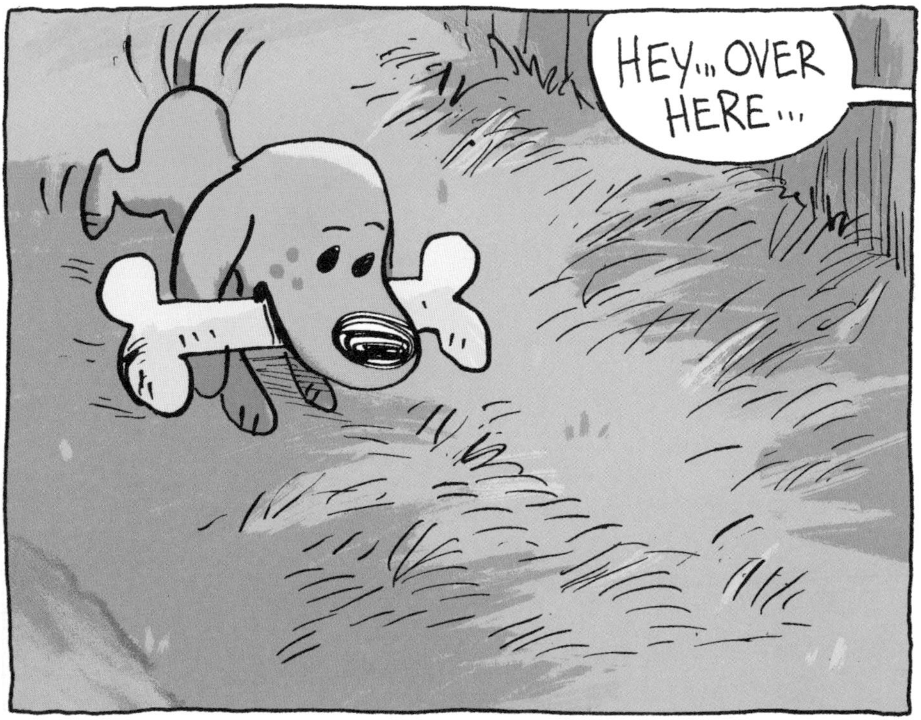
HEY... OVER HERE...

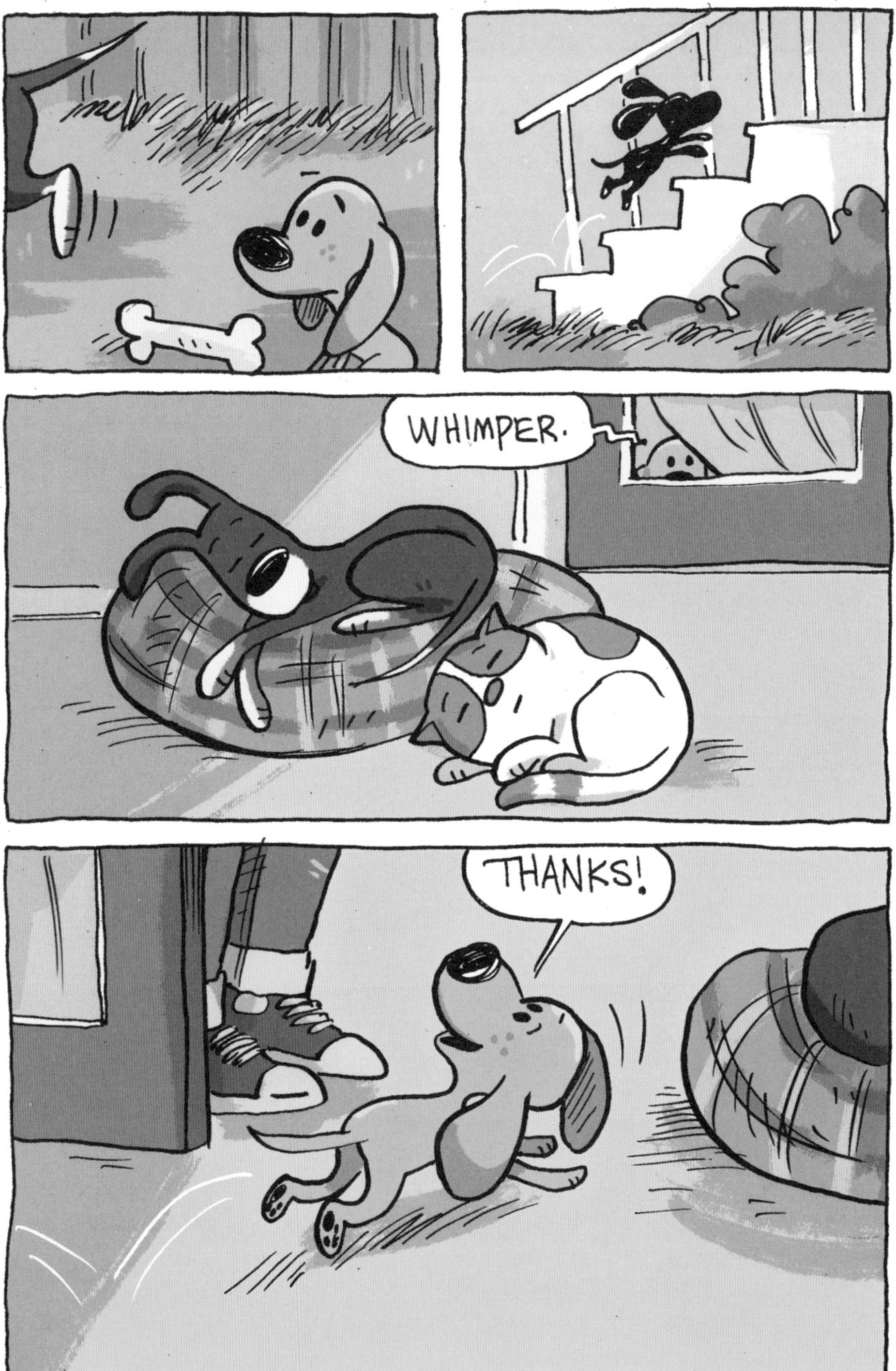
WHIMPER.
THANKS!

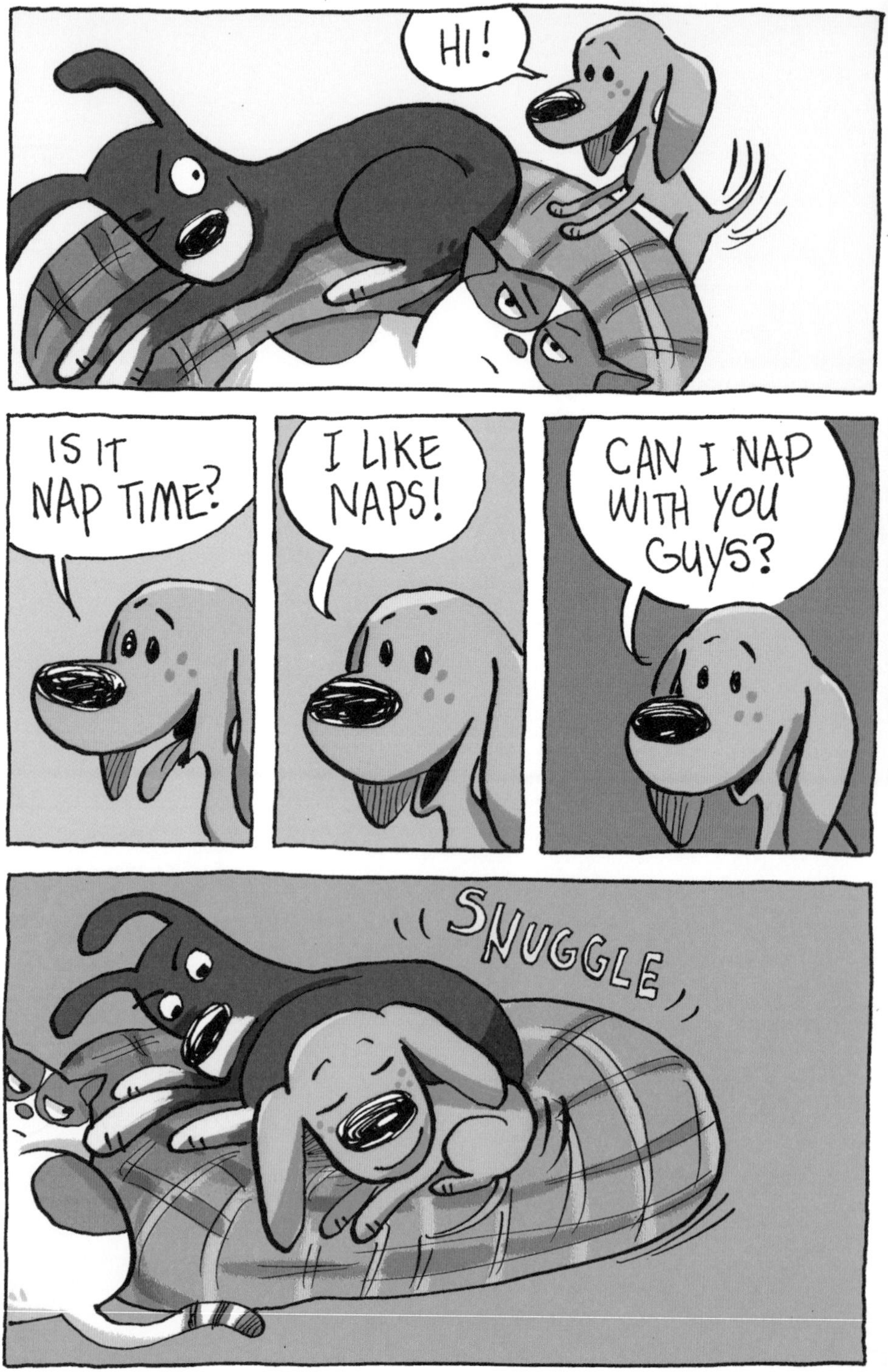
HI!
IS IT NAP TIME?
I LIKE NAPS!
CAN I NAP WITH YOU GUYS?
SNUGGLE

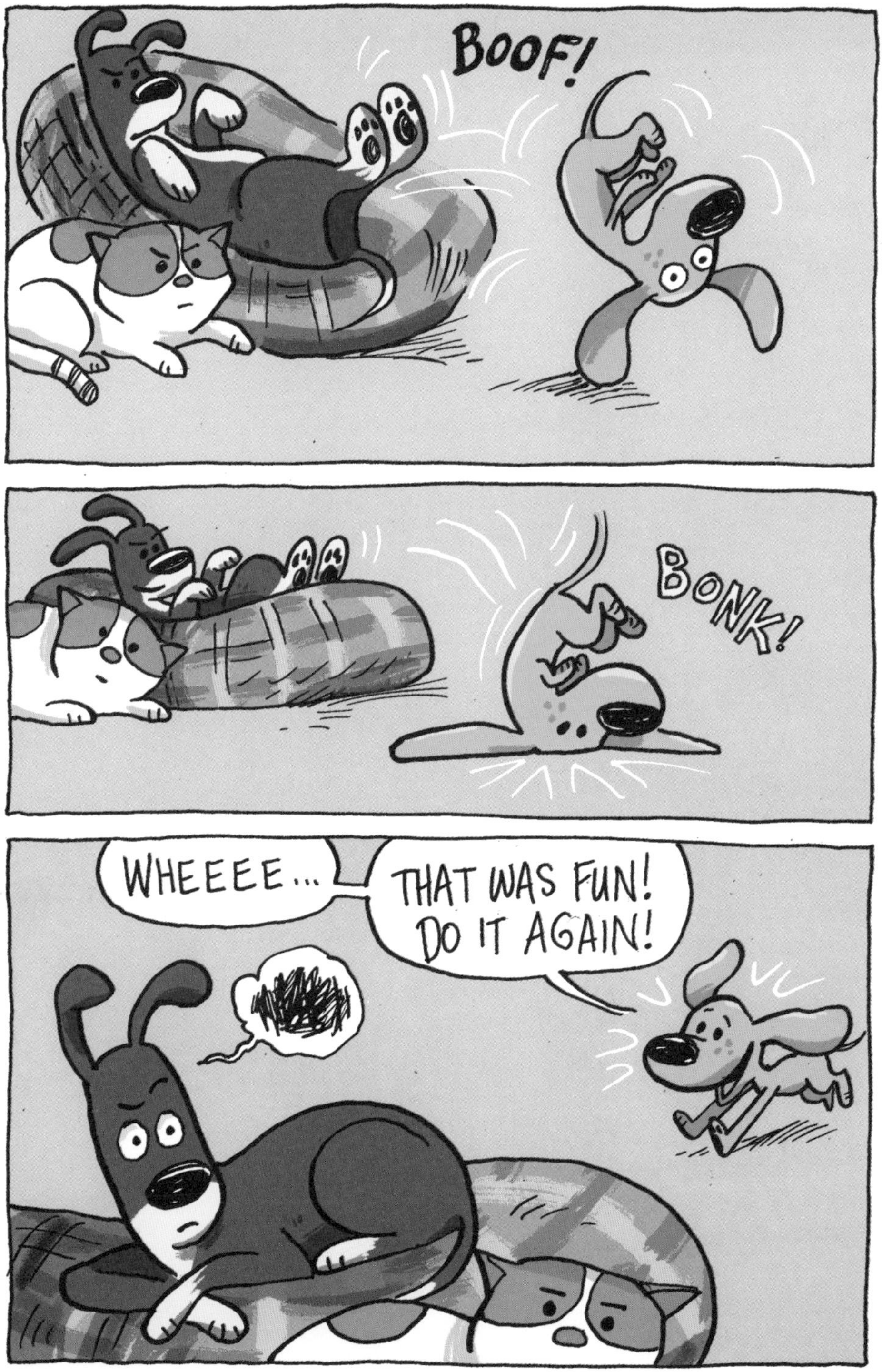
BOOF!
BONK!
WHEEEE...
THAT WAS FUN! DO IT AGAIN!

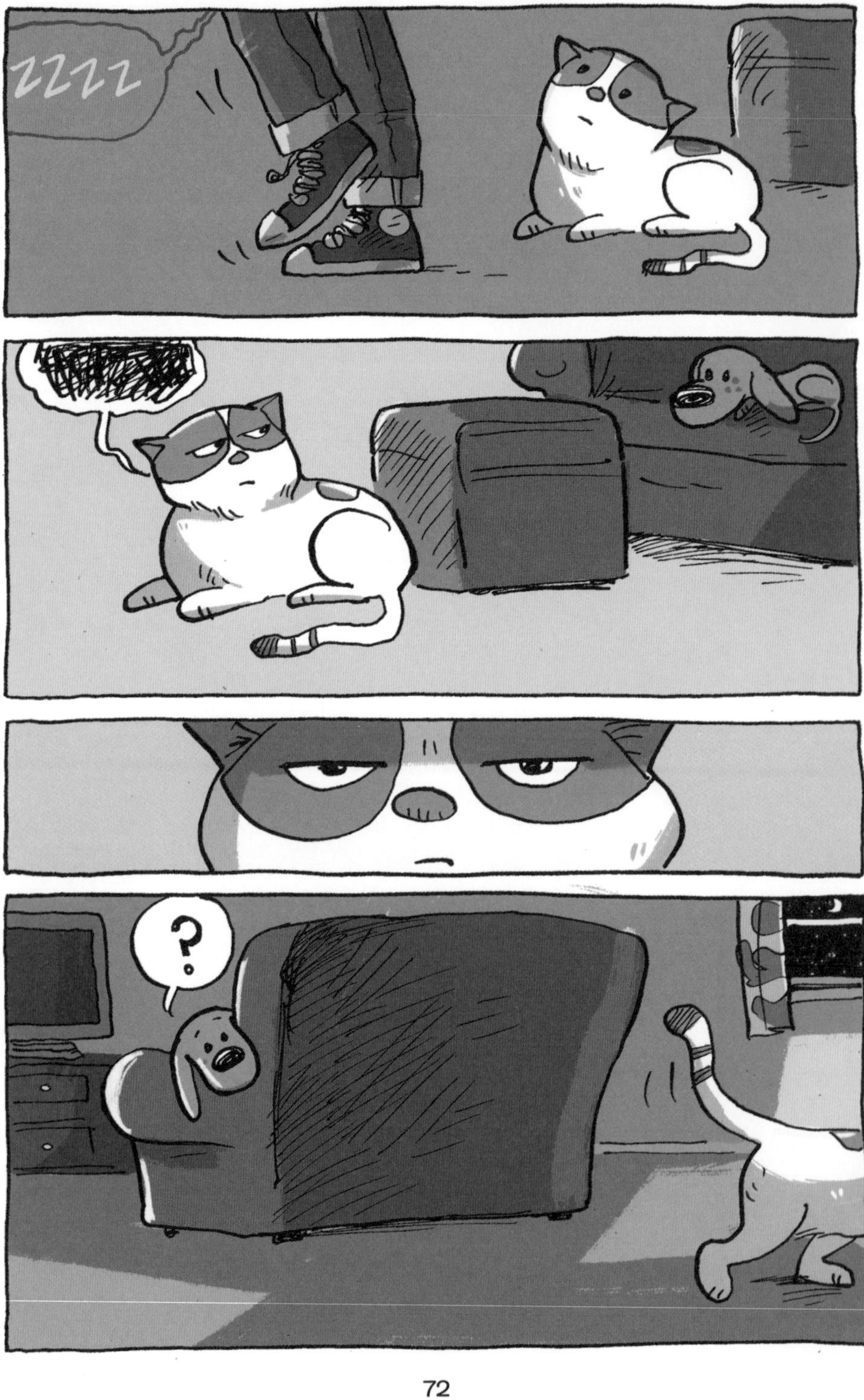
ZZZZ
?

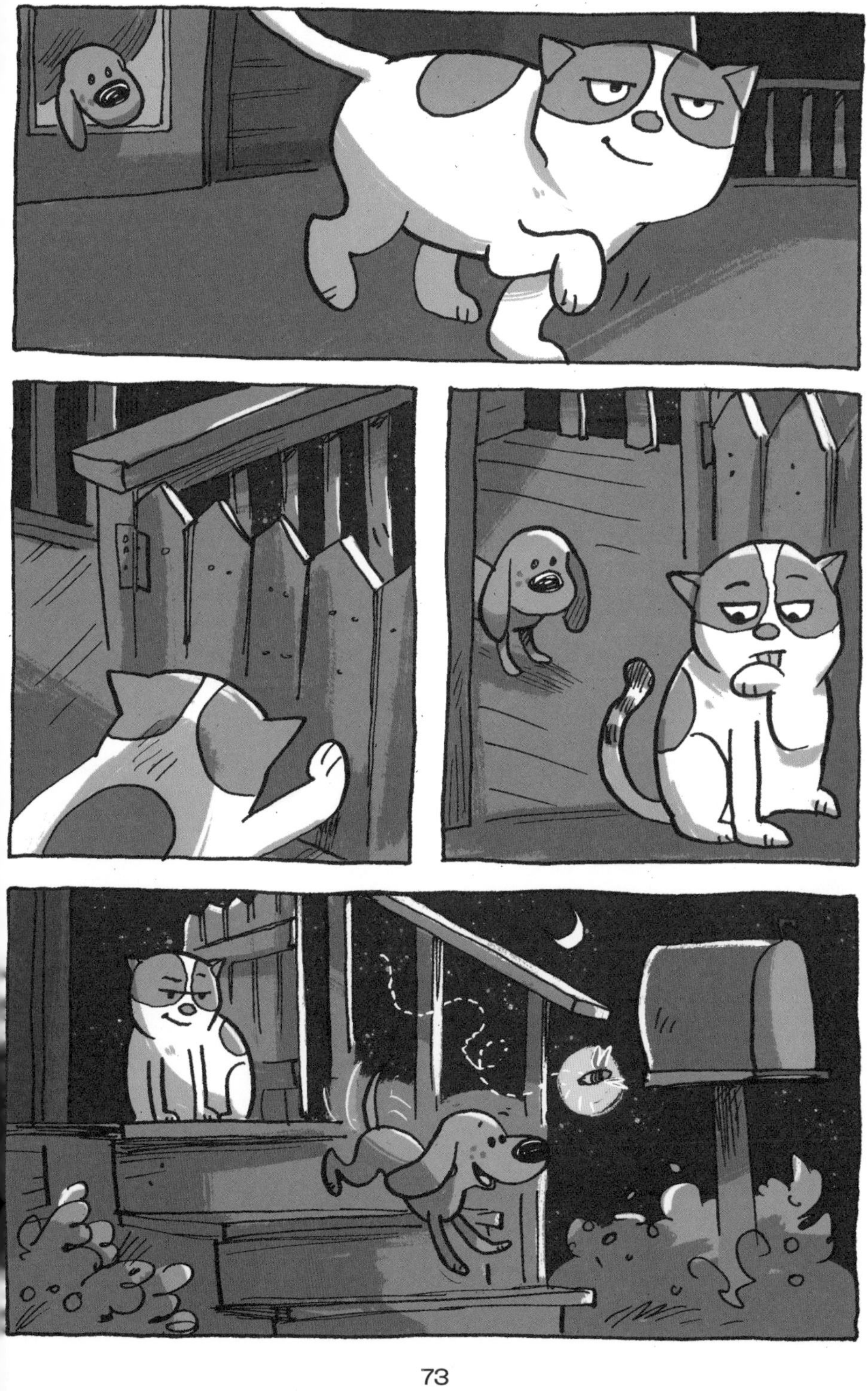

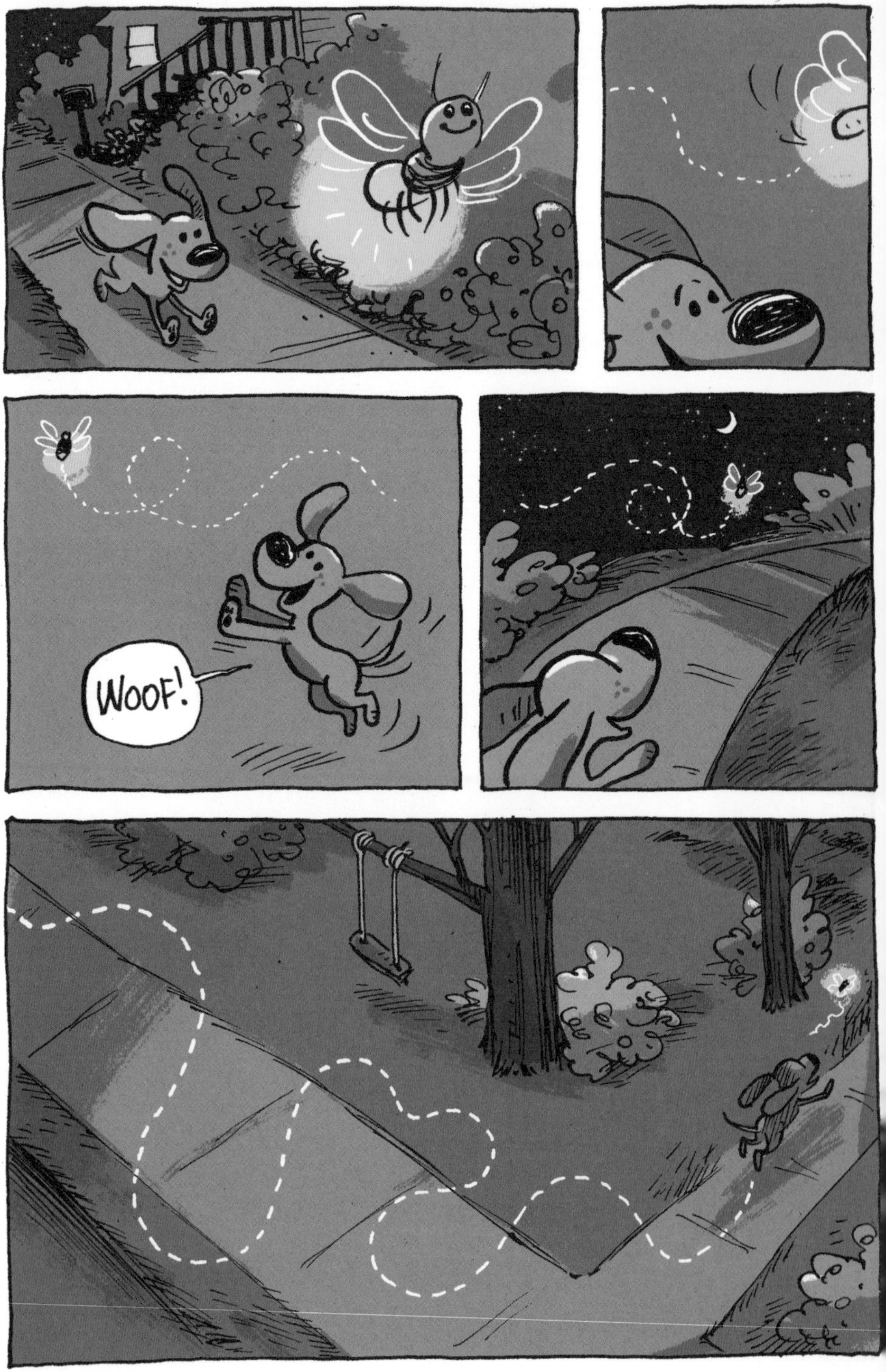
WOOF!

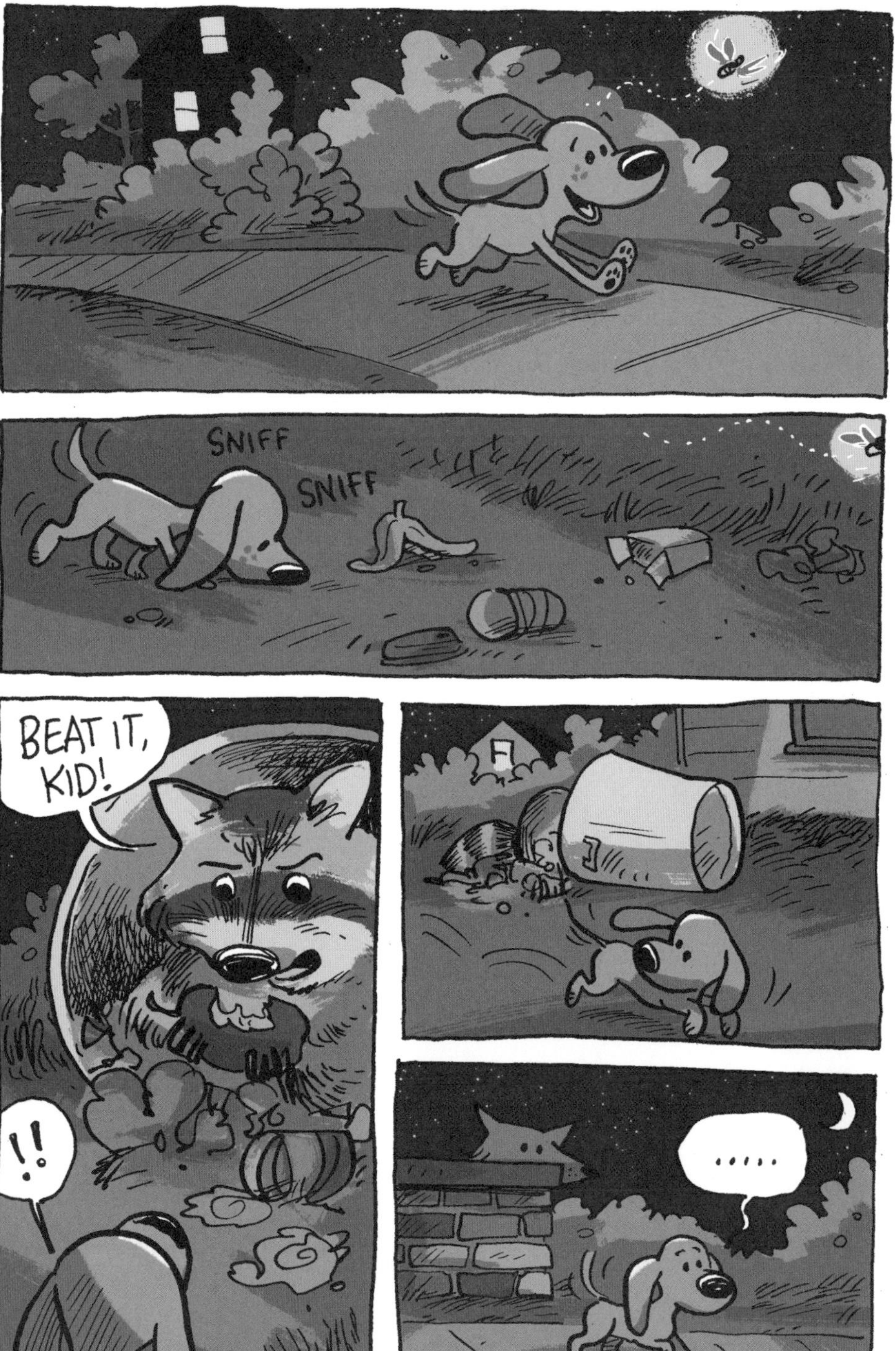

SNIFF
SNIFF
BEAT IT, KID!
!!
.....

79

80

84

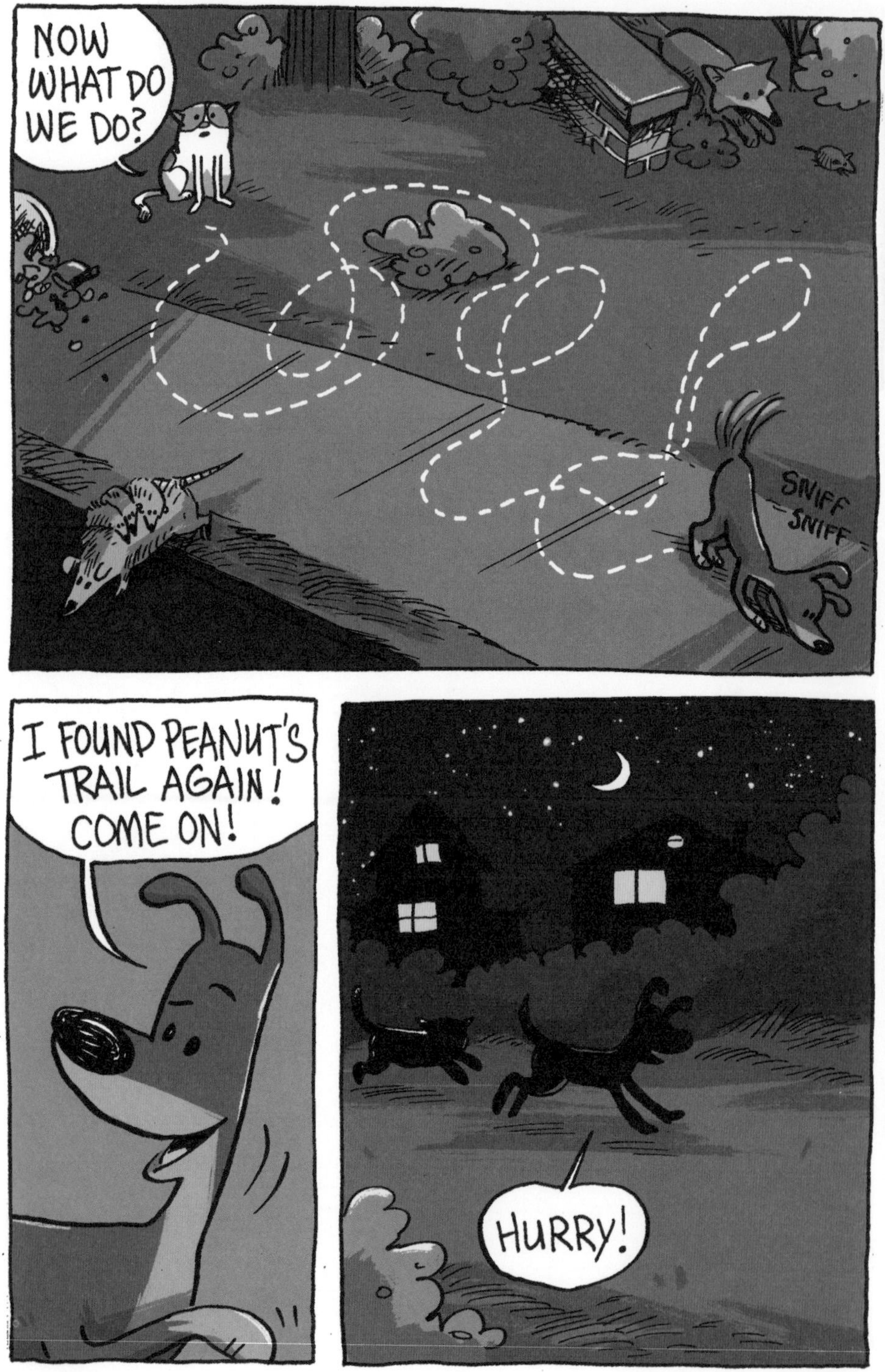
NOW WHAT DO WE DO?
SNIFF SNIFF
I FOUND PEANUT'S TRAIL AGAIN! COME ON!
HURRY!

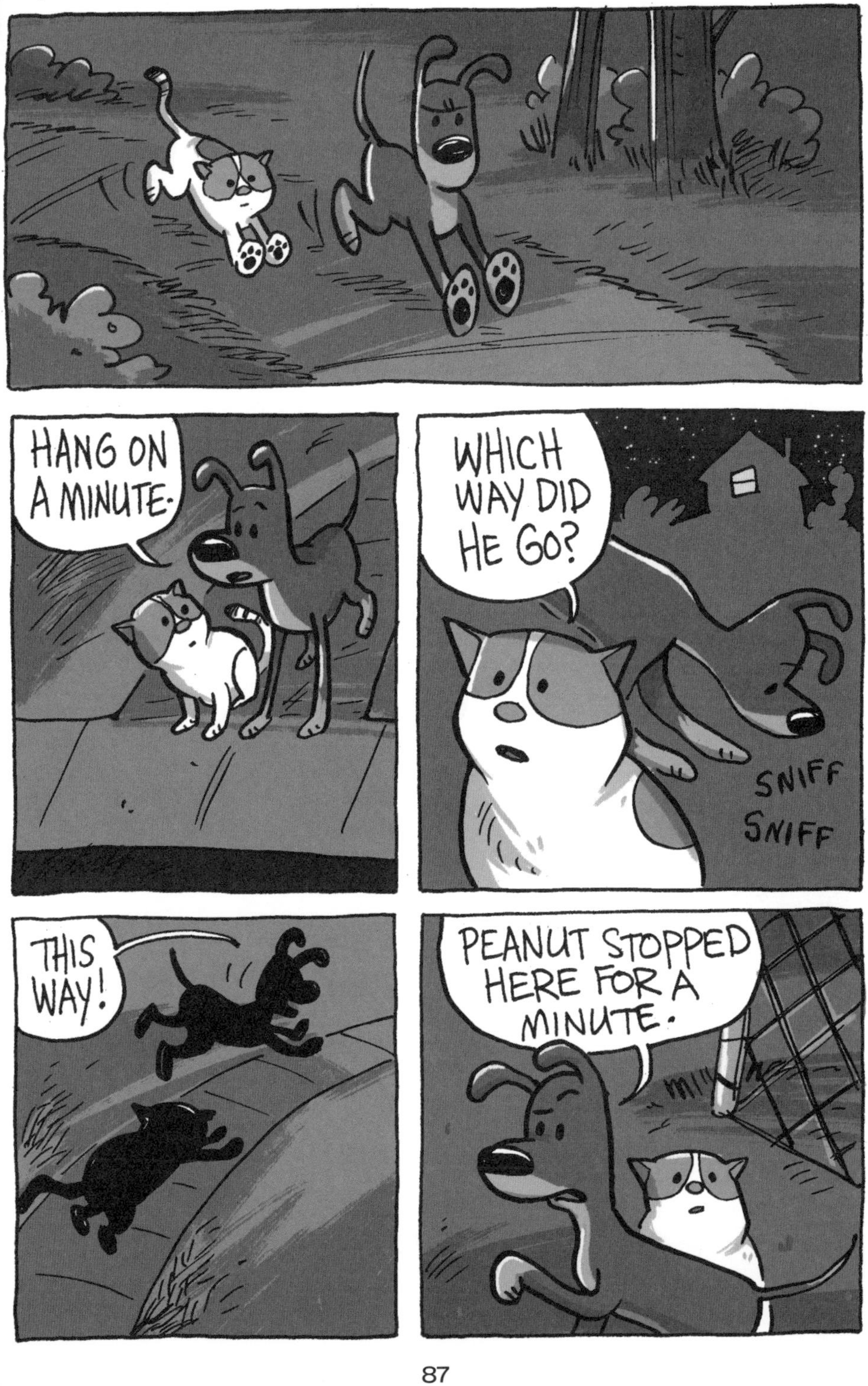
HANG ON A MINUTE.
WHICH WAY DID HE GO?
SNIFF SNIFF
THIS WAY!
PEANUT STOPPED HERE FOR A MINUTE.

90

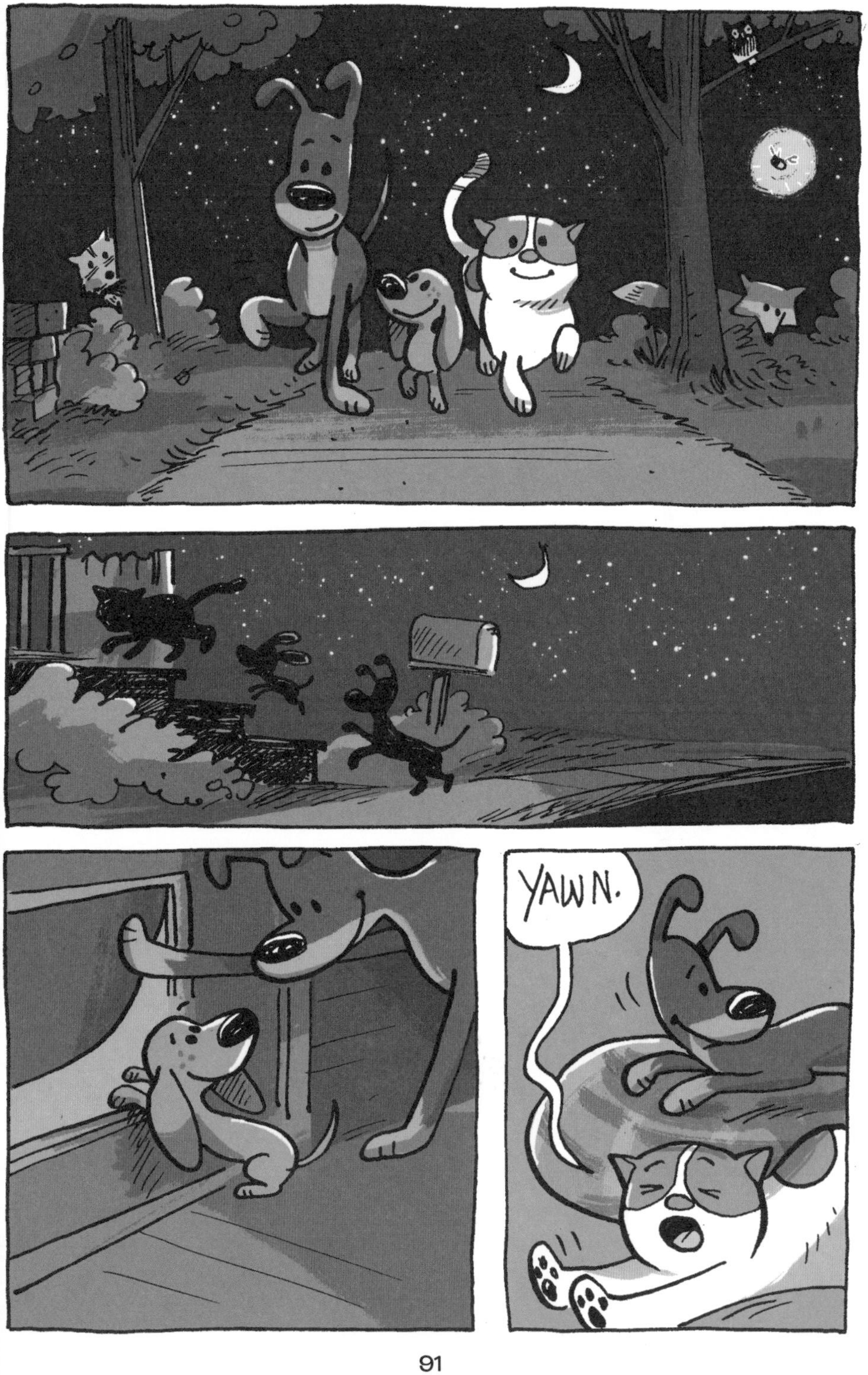
YAWN.

MEET **PAIGE BRADDOCK**

I started drawing comics when I was seven years old. Wiggins, Mississippi, the town I grew up in, was very small. Wiggins didn't have a comic shop or a bookstore. Mostly, I learned about comics by reading the Sunday funnies in the newspaper. My favorite characters to draw were Snoopy, Popeye, and Beetle Bailey. It wasn't long before I started creating my own characters. *Captain Lightning* was the first comics story I wrote and drew. It starred a very clumsy superhero whose cape was always getting snagged on fences and bushes.

Comics have always been one of my favorite things. I majored in illustration in college at the University of Tennessee and later worked as an illustrator for several newspapers. Then I got my dream job: working with Charles M. Schulz at his studio in California. He was the creator of Charlie Brown, Snoopy, and the whole *Peanuts* gang. It's funny how things work out sometimes. Snoopy was one of my all-time favorite characters and now I get to work with him every day.

I've always loved to draw dogs, but when our pet Buddy Barker came to live with us, I started drawing dogs even more often. Buddy was one of the main inspirations for the Peanut, Butter, & Crackers series. Of course, I can't leave out our cat, Otis—who once ate a *whole stick* of butter—and when we added our little dachshund, Charlie, to the mix, we really did have puppy problems!

It's important as artists and writers to figure out what inspires us and to make that part of our story—and *everybody* has a story to tell!

ACKNOWLEDGMENTS

I'd like to offer special thanks to the colorist for this book, Kat Efird. Her colors really brought this story to life in such a vibrant way. Also, big thanks to my editor, Sheila Keenan. I greatly appreciate your sense of humor and your ability to nurture stories. Thank you to my wife, Evelyn, for always suggesting ways to make drawings cuter and funnier.

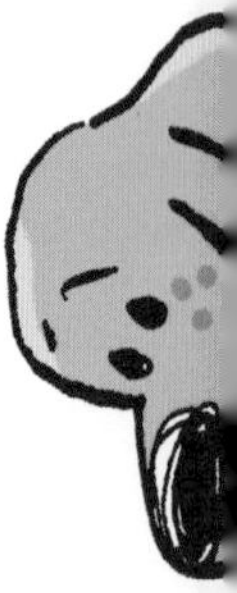

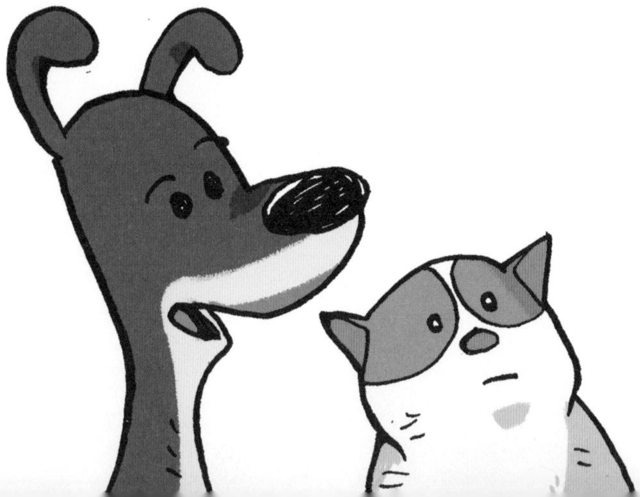